THE SAND CLOCKER

On the 20th of F[...]nada
ship *La Trinida*[...]ty of
Derry Sub-Ac[...]unty
Donegal. I was

On that mem[...]e first
of many artifacts to be discovered. Among other
artifacts salvaged later was a boy's leather boot. That
boot and the boy who wore it were the inspiration for
this tale. I hope you enjoy it.

Jack Scoltock

Jack Scoltock is a native of Derry in Northern
Ireland where he runs a watersports shop. His
adventure stories for young readers include
Jeremy's Adventure, *Quest of the Royal Twins*, *Justine's
Secret Challenge* and *Seek the Enchanted Antlers*; and
his fantasy titles include *Badger Beano and the Magic
Mushroom*, *The Magic Harp* and *The Magic Sword* —
all published by Wolfhound Press.

THE
SAND CLOCKER

SPANISH ARMADA STOWAWAY

Jack Scoltock

WOLFHOUND PRESS

For my son, Jason — with Love.

THANKS

I would like to thank the following:
Father Manus Bradley for the Bishop Réamann O'Gallchóir
Catriona McLaughlin for Irish translation
Mr Jim Doherty and everyone at the Waterside Library who
helped direct me to the research material needed.
The city of Derry Sub-Aqua Club, first of all for the expert tuition
I received when I was learning to dive. For the many happy hours
I spent diving with the club members. For making me an
honorary member.

First published 1996 by
WOLFHOUND PRESS
68 Mountjoy Square
Dublin 1

© 1996 Jack Scoltock

Wolfhound Press receives financial assistance from the Arts Council /
An Chomhairle Ealaíon, Dublin, Ireland
British Library Cataloguing-in-Publication Data
A catalogue record for this book is available from the British Library

ISBN 0-86327-531-1

This book is fiction. All characters, incidents and names have no connection
with any persons living or dead. Any apparent resemblance is purely coin-
cidental.

Cover illustrtaion: Finbarr O'Connor. Cover design: Joe Gervin.
Typesetting: Wolfhound Press

Printed in Ireland by ColourBooks Ltd.

INTRODUCTION

In the 16th century almost all the people in Europe were Christians. By 1580 they were divided into Catholics and Protestants. The Catholics recognised that the Pope in Rome was the leader of the only true religion. The Protestants refused to recognise the Pope as their leader. Elizabeth I of England was a Protestant and she was aware that most of her people in England wanted to be Protestants. When she became Queen of England she became determined to make England a Protestant country.

King Philip of Spain was a devout Catholic. He believed that the Protestant religion was wrong. He believed that by making war on England God would be on his side.

Spain was the strongest Catholic country in Europe and England was the strongest Protestant country. By 1580 King Philip had also annexed Portugal, because King Sebastian of Portugal had died at the age of twenty-four, leaving no heir to the throne. There was little resistance to Spain's forces. King Philip was also related to Sebastian's grandfather and in 1580 he became King of Portugal. He had over thirty thousand of the best soldiers in Europe and few could oppose him.

In 1586 King Phillip made the decision to sail

against England. He did not think his Armada would conquer England but he hoped to persuade Queen Elizabeth to stop executing Catholics and destroying their churches.

The Armada was to carry an army of twenty-five thousand soldiers and slaves, guns and ammunition on one hundred and thirty galleons and galleasses. And so they set sail.

1
ARMADA

'I'm going to join the Armada.'

Those words changed Tomas's life. They were spoken by his cousin Diego as they headed towards the river to hunt for rabbits.

'The Armada!' exclaimed Tomas.

'Yes, I'm going to join the army and sail with her,' said Diego.

Tomas and Diego were more like brothers than cousins. Tomas's parents had died of a fever when he was a baby. His mother's brother, his Uncle Stefano, had brought him to live on his farm outside Lisbon. Tomas's uncle was a gruff hard man, and on the day of Tomas's eighth birthday he was put to work on the farm. He was up at four every morning and worked until eight in the evening. If it had not been for Tomas's cousin, Diego, he would have run away. Diego was fourteen years old, one year older than Tomas. The cousins and everyone else in Portugal had heard about the great Armada that was to set sail for England soon. The Catholic King Philip of Spain had commanded an Armada of one hundred and thirty ships and twenty-five thousand soldiers to get ready to attack England and its ruler, the Protestant Queen Elizabeth.

'But you're far too young to join the army,' said Tomas. 'You have to be sixteen.'

'I can lie, can't I?' said Diego, stopping and expanding his broad chest. He smiled, his white teeth glistening from his swarthy face. He had long straight hair. 'I look sixteen, don't I?'

Tomas had to admit his cousin did look sixteen. He was well built, with muscled arms; not like Tomas, who was tall and slim with dark curly hair.

Diego's next words made him frown.

'You could join too.'

'Me? But I don't look sixteen. I'm only thirteen.'

'Ah, Tomas, you'd pass for sixteen,' said Diego.

As they slipped into the long grass Diego whispered, 'We could walk to Lisbon tonight and enlist together.' He turned and added, smiling, 'Tomas, just think of the adventures we'd have. When we return we'll be heroes and probably rich too.'

Heroes? Rich? thought Tomas. He shocked himself by asking, 'Do you really think I look sixteen?'

His cousin grinned and nodded.

'But ... Diego, what about Uncle; your father? He'd never let us go.'

Diego's grin disappeared. 'He doesn't have to know, does he? Tomas, I don't want to live on the farm all my life. I want to see the world and the best way to do that is to sail with the Armada. Tomas, think about it. We could be in Lisbon tomorrow if we slip out after midnight. The Armada is sailing soon. We could be sailing with her.' Diego studied his cousin's face. 'What do you say?'

Tomas could see that Diego had been thinking about this for some time; probably since they had heard that the Armada was sailing from Lisbon. 'I ... I don't know, Diego,' he answered.

His cousin shrugged his broad shoulders. Then, with a curt 'Come on,' he pushed into the taller grass. 'Let's get over to the clearing.'

Soon they were slipping as silently as they could towards the clearing near the edge of the river. Tomas buzzed with excitement. Diego's words came to him. 'The Armada is sailing soon. We could be sailing with her.' The light wind blowing through the grass, cooling his sweating brow, suddenly made him shiver. He followed Diego for about forty yards.

Suddenly, with a hiss, Diego stopped. He signalled for Tomas to crouch lower; then he reached back. Tomas crawled towards him and slipped one of the three crude arrows he carried into Diego's hand. The cousins peered through the grass into the small clearing. They could see several rabbits feeding on the shorter grass a few yards from one of the biggest rabbit holes. Tomas held his breath as Diego slowly rose to his knees. The veins stood out on his forearms and the bow quivered as he took aim. The 'Thwack!' as the arrow shot from the bow alerted the rabbits, but it was too late for one of them. The arrow had ripped through its back leg. As it lay screaming the other rabbits disappeared into the hole.

With a whoop of delight Diego dropped the bow

and jumped to his feet. In seconds he was beside the terrified creature. When Tomas reached him Diego was holding the kicking rabbit by its long ears. With his other hand Diego pulled a home-made knife from his belt. He was about to draw the blade across the rabbit's throat when he glanced at Tomas. Grinning, he handed Tomas the knife, saying, 'You do it, Tomas. Slit its throat.'

The words shocked Tomas. The rabbit struggled and cried out again. Tomas stared at the knife. He couldn't move. He had hidden from his cousin how he hated to see the tiny creatures killed. Tomas looked at the rabbit's glazed fearful eyes. Suddenly it stopped struggling. Diego frowned. The rabbit was dead. With a grunt of disappointment he threw it to the ground.

'Give me the knife,' he rasped. He glared at Tomas.

Tomas turned away as his cousin quickly skinned the rabbit. When he was finished Tomas said, 'I'm sorry, Diego, but I couldn't kill it. I couldn't ...'

Diego stared at him. 'A rabbit!' he exclaimed. 'You couldn't kill a rabbit. Madre-de-Dios, what use are you going to be to the Armada when you couldn't even kill a rabbit? Tomas, you'll be killing *men*. How will you fare when you have to kill an Englishman?'

'Oh,' said Tomas quickly, 'I could kill an Englishman all right.'

Diego stared at him. 'You couldn't kill a rabbit but you could kill a man ...' Suddenly he began to laugh. 'You couldn't kill ... ha, ha, ha ... a rabbit ... ha, ha, ha ...'

Now Tomas began to laugh. Their laughter echoed across the calm river they would never see again. Flies and other insects, sensing the rabbit's bloody carcass, began to wing towards it.

Later, as Tomas and Diego ate a rabbit stew made with some vegetables they had stolen on the way home, they worked out a plan. By then Tomas was determined to go with his cousin. They decided to slip away after midnight. Diego kept some cooked rabbit to eat on the long walk to Lisbon.

That night they met at the end of the dirt track that led to the chicken house. The bright moonlight lit up the whole countryside as they headed across three wide fields to the road that led to Lisbon.

'Well, Tomas,' said Diego when they reached the road. 'There's no turning back now.' He looked around and sighed happily. 'We'll always remember this night.'

'Yes,' whispered Tomas as bats swooped past them. Suddenly he was frightened, but as they walked he listened to his cousin telling him that nothing could harm them if they stayed together.

'We'll always be together,' vowed Diego.

They were to be parted sooner than they thought.

2
ENLISTING

They reached the bustling city of Lisbon around eight in the morning. Lisbon was loud with vendors selling their wares. There were soldiers, sailors and women everywhere. Some of them were still drunk from a heavy night's drinking in the taverns. Many were sleeping it off in doorways or slumped against walls. There was an excitement in the air you could cut with a knife, and Tomas and Diego were excited yet apprehensive as they headed towards the harbour. On the way they saw a group of boozy-eyed soldiers emerging from a tavern. One of them cursed loudly as he fell over a stool. The other soldiers laughed at him.

'I'll ask one of them the way to the enlisting office,' whispered Diego.

By then Tomas was half regretting his decision to go with his cousin. He watched as Diego stopped a soldier. Suddenly the soldier pushed him away. 'Enlisting office!' he exclaimed. 'What would a sapling like you want with the enlisting office?'

'I'm not a sapling!' shouted Diego, reaching for his dagger. 'I'm sixteen.' He nodded at Tomas. 'We're both sixteen. We've come to Lisbon to join the army and sail with the Armada.'

The soldier squinted at Tomas, then said to

Diego, 'You say you're sixteen, boy.' He studied Diego. 'Aye, you might well be. But that one,' he nodded at Tomas, 'Never. He's twelve if he's a day.'

Tomas's face grew red. One of the soldiers said something he couldn't quite make out and the others laughed. The soldier Diego had spoken to pushed him out of the way, then began to head after the others to an adjacent street. As he did he turned. 'You'll find the enlisting office down near the harbour. But I would advise both of you to go home and forget about enlisting.'

Diego scowled after him. When he came over to Tomas he said, 'Come on, Tomas, let's get to the harbour. We'll soon find the enlisting office.'

When they came near the harbour they saw dozens of tall masts peeking above the rooftops. In the narrow paved streets around the harbour there were more sailors and soldiers. Everyone seemed to be in a feverish, excited mood. Their excitement caught the cousins in its grip as they made their way along crowded streets.

Diego stopped several soldiers to ask for directions to the enlisting office. Eventually, guided by the little he received, the cousins found themselves at the bottom of a long street. Diego looked up it. 'The enlisting office should be near the top,' he said.

They walked up the street, which was lined with small balconies, several of which held huge pots overflowing with colourful masses of flowers. On one of the balconies they saw two young girls throwing flowers down to four soldiers who were shouting entreaties up to them. Diego smiled as one of the flowers landed on his head.

Doubt began to fill Tomas as they drew near the top of the street. What will I do, he thought, if Diego is allowed to enlist and I'm not? His worries increased as they came to a doorway. The top half was open. Above the opening were the words: Recruiting Office.

Diego smiled at Tomas; then, taking a deep breath, he pushed the bottom half of the door open and led the way inside.

A fat, grizzled sergeant wearing a uniform sat behind a low desk. The room smelled of stale wine, and there was a half-empty bottle on the table. Through an open door behind the sergeant, Tomas and Diego could see six soldiers drinking wine and playing some card game, arguing loudly. The sergeant scowled at the cousins. His tunic was open at the neck and the brass buttons strained around his portly stomach. 'What do you want?' he growled.

Tomas gulped.

'We've come to join King Philip's army, sir,' said Diego, sticking his chest out.

The sergeant studied him. 'You have, have you.' He looked at Tomas, then at Diego. 'What age are you, boy?'

'Sixteen ... and a half,' said Diego, glancing at Tomas.

The sergeant gave a sort of snort. Then he looked at Tomas. 'And you, boy?'

'W... what?'

'Age, boy? What age are you?' snapped the sergeant.

'S... s ... sixteen, sir,' stammered Tomas.

The sergeant's small eyes seemed to burn into Tomas. He looked at Diego, who nodded and smiled, trying to look confident but failing in his deceit. The sergeant studied both of them again. A shout from one of the soldiers behind made him turn. 'Be quiet in there!' he bellowed. He looked at Diego. 'Right,' he said, pushing a sheet of dog-eared paper across the desk at Diego. 'Sign on the bottom.'

Diego smiled at Tomas in triumph; but remembering, he said, 'Sir, I can't write.'

The sergeant scowled at him.

'But I can fight,' said Diego quickly. He raised his arms and flexed his muscles.

The sergeant allowed a tiny smile to change his face. 'I bet you can,' he said quietly. He pointed to the form. 'Just make your mark.'

Smiling, Diego dipped a feathered quill into a pot of red ink and scratched a crude X on the bottom of the form.

The sergeant pulled it towards him. He held it up to his face, looking at the cousins as he breathed hard on the X to dry the ink. Then he placed the form on top of a few others to his right. Nodding to the door behind him, he said, 'You'll find a uniform in the back. Put one on that's a bit large for you.'

Diego frowned. 'Large?'

'You're still growing, aren't you? Uniforms are scarce. You only get one and it has to last you a long time,' explained the soldier.

Diego smiled at Tomas. His smile vanished when he heard the sergeant say to Tomas, 'Now, you boy, be off. Come back in a few years when you're old enough to join the King's army.'

'What?' gasped Diego.

Tomas gaped at the sergeant. 'But ...' He looked at his cousin.

'I said be off with you!' roared the sergeant, his stubby fingers curled into fists.

'But, sir, Tomas and I are going to fight the English together.'

The sergeant shrugged his shoulders.

Diego scowled. 'If Tomas isn't going then neither am I.'

At this the sergeant pushed the table away and rose to his feet. It was only then the cousins realised how big he was.

'Boy,' he growled to Diego, 'you're a soldier in King Philip's army now. You've made your mark and enlisted. Now get into that room and select a uniform or I'll have you dragged off to jail for disobeying an order.'

'But ...' began Diego.

By now the other soldiers had gathered at the doorway. They were grinning.

'Did you hear me, soldier!' roared the sergeant, banging his fist on the table.

At this Diego drew himself up to his full height. His face was blazing as he shouted, 'If Tomas isn't going to be allowed to enlist then neither am I ...'

The sergeant's eyes bulged as he roared, 'You've already enlisted!' Turning to the soldiers, he shouted, 'Take this dog and fit him out with a uniform. When you have done that escort him to the galleon *Trinidad Valencera*.'

Tomas stared as his struggling cousin was dragged into the room. Inside he could hear the curses of the soldiers and his cousin's angry protestations.

'Boy,' snarled the sergeant, gathering the forms up and tapping them neatly together, 'I told you to go. Now do as you're told or I'll have you thrown into jail.'

Tomas's eyes filled with tears. 'But, sir, couldn't you let me enlist?' he cried. 'I can fight as well as Diego.'

The sergeant's look softened. 'I've no doubt that's true, boy, but you're not the age to enlist and don't tell me you're sixteen.'

'Please ...'

The sergeant glared at Tomas. 'Get out!' he roared suddenly. He shoved his face towards Tomas. 'I said get out!'

Slowly Tomas backed out of the office. What am I going to do now? he thought dismally.

3
LOADING BARRELS

Half an hour later seven soldiers came marching out of the enlisting office. One of them was Diego. His face was grim as he marched between the others. Though his suit was much too big for him, Tomas, watching from a doorway, couldn't help envying him. He looks like a real soldier, thought Tomas. He is a real soldier. He sniffed as his eyes filled with tears. What am I going to do? I can't go back to Uncle's farm; not without Diego. Uncle will flay me alive.

Keeping Diego and the other soldiers in sight, Tomas followed them up to the top of the street and around the corner. The soldiers kept up a good pace as they marched down the street. Other soldiers and sailors crowded the narrow street, hindering Tomas's progress. He had to jump up and down to keep his cousin in sight.

Near the bottom of the street a crowd of soldiers and sailors were arguing. They halted Tomas's progress for a few seconds and he lost sight of Diego. When he pushed through them and around the corner he stopped. His eyes widened. He was in a wide plaza; it was packed with sailors, soldiers and many young women. Tomas panicked. Where was Diego? Pushing through the crowd, he tried to catch sight of his cousin, but it was impossible. 'Diego!' he shouted. 'Diego, where are you? Oh, where is he?' he cried. 'I have to find him.'

An hour later, after frantically searching the plaza and the adjacent streets, Tomas gave up. He sat on the edge of a water fountain, numbly watching the crowds as they thronged about the plaza. I have to find him, he thought. But where?

Then he remembered: the sergeant had ordered the soldiers to take Diego to the galleon *Trinidad Valencera*.

Soon he was walking along the edge of the quay. Rows of galleons and galleasses, the smaller ships, were docked along the wooden quay. The gangways leading up to the lower decks were busy with men carrying baskets of fresh food and vegetables. Dockers were rolling huge barrels of water up broader gangways.

Ahead of him Tomas saw a huge bronze cannon being hoisted right up over the top deck and lowered into the hold. He stood watching as several dockers, helped by sailors, tied hemp ropes around an eighteen-foot-long carriage which was to hold the cannon. Shortly it too was being hoisted aboard.

A few seconds later he heard the marching of feet behind him. A group of about twenty soldiers passed him and marched up one of the broad gangways and into a ship.

As he walked slowly along the edge of the quay Tomas looked for the name. '*Valencera*,' he muttered.

Looking around, Tomas saw an old man nearby unloading vegetables from a cart. Going over to him, he asked, 'Is the Armada sailing soon?'

'On the next tide,' replied the man.

'The next tide!' gasped Tomas. 'When is that?'

'First light tomorrow,' replied the man.

'In the morning,' exclaimed Tomas. 'I must find Diego. I must find the *Valencera*.' He hurried along the harbour.

He could see the *Gran Grifon*, the *San Marcos*, the *Gerona*, the *San Felipe* and a huge galleon called the *San Salvador*, but no *Valencera*. Tomas could not write, but he read a little, and he knew that the word *Valencera* began with a V. He had seen his cousin's youngest sister write her name, Verona, and he remembered what the V at the beginning looked like.

The men loading the ships ran up and down the gangways like ants. Tomas was shoved aside several times as he walked in a daze between the edge of the quay and rows of water barrels. Once he tripped over a wooden bollard and almost tumbled into the water. As he staggered back he heard his name being called.

'Tomas! Tomas, up here! Tomas!'

Recognising his cousin's voice, Tomas looked along the decks of the ship. From a group of soldiers who lined the decks, a hand was waving at him.

'Diego!' he screamed. He waved frantically.

'Tomas, tell Father where I've gone!' shouted Diego.

Tomas caught a glimpse of his cousin's pale face. He looked frightened. Just then an officer came running up the gangway. 'Down to the lower deck,' he ordered. 'Move!'

The soldiers disappeared.

'Diego! Diego!' shouted Tomas. He clambered up onto one of the barrels. From there he could clearly see the name of the galleon: '*La Trinidad Valencera.*' He looked along the decks. He could not see any soldiers.

'Hey, boy, get down from there!'

A docker stood below Tomas. Two other dock workers were rolling a barrel to the bottom of the gangway. The man who had called out, and another man, were waiting to do the same with the barrel Tomas was standing on. The dockers were bare-footed and wore light pantaloons. Two of them wore head-bands.

Tomas said 'Sorry,' and jumped down. He watched as the sweating men pulled the barrel easily over onto its side, then began to roll it towards the gangway of the *Valencera*. At the top the other two dockers waited until the barrel was trundled up the gangway into the ship; then they hurried down for another barrel.

Tomas looked behind. There were about a hundred barrels to be loaded.

I must get on board, he thought. If I can only hide on the *Valencera* till she sails ... The captain will hardly turn back if I'm found when we're out at sea. They'd have to make me a soldier. 'They'd have to,' he muttered.

When two of the men came down Tomas went over to them. As they were heaving the barrel onto its side, Tomas asked, 'May I help?'

The stoutest of the dockers wiped sweat from his brow. His arms were as thick as trunks and knotted with muscles. 'Help?' he said.

'Yes, may I help you load the barrels onto the ships?'

'You may if you wish, boy,' said the man, grinning at his mate. 'But you will not be paid. Will he Pablo?'

'Oh, I don't want pay,' said Tomas brightly. 'It would be an honour to help load food for our gallant soldiers.'

The stout man studied Tomas, then looked at his mate. Pablo shrugged his shoulders. 'Well, if you want to help that's fine with us, but it's hard work and remember, there will be no pay. Now do you still want to help?'

'Yes,' said Tomas, smiling. 'I don't mind hard work.'

Soon he was between the dockers, helping them trundle the heavy barrels up the gangway. It was hard work and it wasn't long before Tomas was sweating and hungry. He remembered that he and Diego had eaten the last of the rabbit meat an hour before they reached Lisbon.

An hour and a quarter later the dock workers stopped for a break. When the four men and Tomas were sitting in the shade of the rest of the barrels, the stout man handed Tomas a piece of dry bread and cheese.

'Thanks,' said Tomas, cramming the bread into his mouth. Pablo handed him a bottle of red wine. Tomas took a swig, coughed a few times, and handed it back to the grinning man.

As they rested one of the men tapped the barrel he was leaning against. 'We would have had many more barrels to load if it hadn't been for that cursed Englishman, Drake.'

'Aye, you're right, Miguel,' said the stout man. 'How many barrels did he burn at Cadiz last year?'

'I heard it was thousands,' said Pablo.

The stout man studied the barrel beside him. 'These barrels are made from poor quality wood. Some of them aren't properly cured. The water won't stay fresh in them for long.'

'It should do until they reach England,' said Pablo. 'I wish I could go with the Armada.'

'Me too,' said the youngest of the four men.

'And me,' said Tomas.

The dockers looked at him.

'You're much too young, boy,' said the stout man. 'Except maybe for being a sand clocker.' He grinned as Pablo added, 'And pushing barrels.'

Tomas frowned. 'What's a sand clocker?'

'A boy who turns the sand clock every half hour on board ship,' answered the stout man. 'My nephew is a sand clocker on board the *San Felipe*.'

Tomas's frown deepened. 'I don't understand. Why does the clock have to be turned at all?'

'You see,' explained the stout man, 'the captain of the ship needs to know the time on a long journey. He also estimates what speed his ship is going. When he compares the speed and the time passed, he has a fair idea how far he has travelled.'

Tomas grew excited. 'And you say I could be a sand clocker?'

'I'm sure you could,' said the stout man. 'You're young enough. But every ship would have a sand clocker by now.'

Tomas's heart was pounding as he looked at the *Valencera*. I must get on board, he thought. I'll have to stow away, and soon. He looked along the line of galleons, then at the barrels. It won't take long before all the barrels are loaded, he thought.

'Right,' grunted the stout man, pulling himself to his feet by holding onto the top of a barrel. 'Let's get the rest of these barrels on board, then we can have a long siesta.'

As the fifteenth barrel was being loaded Tomas decided to make his move. He knew he might not have another chance. As the stout man, Pablo and Tomas pushed the heavy barrel over the top of the gangway onto the deck, his heart was pounding. His heartbeat speeded up even more as they rolled the barrel towards two sailors waiting by the hatch that led down to the hold. Tomas glanced at the nearest lifeboat; he had decided the covered lifeboat would be the best place to hide.

As they walked back to the top of the gangway Tomas held back. With one eye on the sailors and the other on the dockers, who were already walking down the gangway, Tomas held his breath. When the sailors disappeared below, he slipped towards the lifeboat. He looked around;

there was no one in sight. As he quickly climbed into the lifeboat and pulled the cover behind him, he thought: there's no turning back now.

He crawled to the middle of the lifeboat and curled up on a tangle of thick ropes and belay pins. His heart was still pounding, and he was frightened as well as excited. He prayed that he would not be found until the galleon was well out to sea.

Somehow he managed to drift off to sleep. He woke shortly before dark and lay awake and hungry for the next seven or eight hours. About an hour before dawn he fell asleep again.

4
AT SEA

Loud cheering woke him. He could feel the movement of the ship. Crawling to the edge of the lifeboat, he peered out. The ship was moving away from the crowded quay. Sailors were busy following shouted instructions from their captain. From where he hid Tomas could see waving soldiers gathered along the deck; he looked for Diego but couldn't see him.

As the wind filled the sails the ship gave a sudden lurch forward. Through the narrow crack between the cover and the lifeboat he could see two other ships with sails raised heading out to sea. Tomas smiled. Soon he would be joining Diego. At last they were on their way to England! All he had to do now was to stay hidden until the ship was well out to sea.

Suddenly his stomach rumbled, and he realised he had had no food for almost a full day. Crawling to the middle of the lifeboat, he lay back. He estimated that it was around seven o'clock. By mid-day the ship would be well out to sea. When it is I will go to the captain and declare myself, he thought. His stomach rumbled again. The slap of the sails, the cry of gulls, the shouts of the captain and the wind whistling around the ship made him drowsy, and he dozed off.

He was woken by noise and a dazzle of bright light as the cover of the lifeboat was pulled back. Tomas blinked at two astonished sailors. The bigger of them grabbed him by the ankle and dragged him to the edge of the lifeboat.

'A stowaway!' exclaimed the burly sailor. 'Captain won't be pleased.'

The sailor had a small scar above his left eye. He had thick curly black hair and wore two earrings.

The grip on Tomas's ankle was excruciating and he kicked out with his free leg. The sailor grabbed it and snarled, 'Quit that, boy, or I'll pitch you overboard. Sharks will make short work of you.'

Tomas, frightened, allowed himself to be pulled out of the lifeboat. He hit the deck on his back.

'Manuel,' said the burly sailor, gripping Tomas by the left arm. 'You get the ropes from the lifeboat. I'll take this one to the captain.'

Struggling half-heartedly, Tomas was led along the rolling deck to a door. At least, he thought, we're well out to sea. They'll hardly turn back because of me.

Knocking on the door, the sailor shouted, 'Seaman Rodrigo to see the captain urgently.' Turning, he grinned at Tomas, showing a gap where two front teeth were missing. 'Captain De Salto will probably have you keel-hauled.'

The door opened and a balding middle-aged man stared at Tomas.

'Found him in the lifeboat, captain,' said Rodrigo, relaxing his grip on Tomas's arm.

Wincing, Tomas rubbed it. 'Sir ...' he began.

'Quiet!' shouted Rodrigo, raising his hand to strike Tomas.

'Let him speak,' said the captain. His eyes burned into Tomas's pale face. 'Why did you stow away on my ship?'

'To fight the English, sir,' answered Tomas. 'The sergeant at the enlisting office said I was too young to join the army. My cousin Diego was allowed to join. He's on this ship.' Tomas straightened and stuck out his chest. 'I can fight, sir. I can do anything, only please don't keel-haul me.' Tomas wondered what keel-hauling was.

The captain's eyes twinkled. 'Keel-haul you?' he said, looking at Rodrigo. 'No, nothing as drastic as that.'

Just then the first mate, a thin man with greying hair, who was called Juan, staggered across the deck towards them. He gave Tomas a glance, then said to De Salto, 'Captain, there's over a hundred soldiers seasick. There will be many more. Two sand clockers and three of the crew are also sick.'

The captain frowned. He was about to go with Juan; then, remembering Tomas, he asked him, 'What's your name?'

'Tomas, sir. Tomas Arraganzo.'

The captain said to Rodrigo, 'Take Tomas to the cook. He can help out in the galley until we land.' He turned to go.

'Sir,' said Tomas quickly. 'I can keep the time.' He didn't like the idea of spending the long voyage in the ship's galley.

'We'll need someone to relieve Pedro, sir,' said Juan. 'There's no telling when the other two sand clockers will be fit enough to take their shift.'

Captain De Salto studied Tomas. 'Do you know what a sand clock is, Tomas?'

'Yes, sir,' lied Tomas. 'I can look after it. You can depend on me. I'll ... I'll do anything, sir.'

De Salto turned to Rodrigo. 'Take Tomas to Pedro. Tell Pedro he is to show Tomas the principles of the sand clock.' To Tomas he said, 'You had better learn quickly, and if you get seasick I will keel-haul you.'

As they stumbled across the deck the first mate said something to the captain and they both laughed.

'Come, boy,' growled Rodrigo, reaching to grab Tomas's arm. 'Count yourself lucky. There are many on board who are not used to the sea, especially when it is as rough as this; and it will get much stormier before this journey is over. The soldiers below are not used to the sea. Many more will get sick. By the time we reach England there won't be many of them fit to walk, never mind fight the English.'

As Rodrigo led Tomas along the deck Tomas could see many ships in front and along each side of the *Valencera*. Galleons and galleasses stretched as far as the eye could see.

The wind and the spray from the waves pounding the *Valencera* made it impossible to walk in a straight line. Several times Tomas stumbled and would have fallen if it had not been for

Rodrigo's grip on his arm. As they climbed a row of steps Tomas heard a voice above sing out:

One glass is gone, another's a-filling.
More sand shall run, if God is willing.
To my God let us pray, to make safe our way;
And His Mother, Our Lady, who prays for us all,
To save us from tempest and threatening squall.

Tomas saw a tall boy with brown hair standing on deck, near where a sailor wrestled with the ship's steering wheel; the boy was the one who had been singing. Beside him was a strange-looking glass with bulbous ends. Tomas could see sand running from the top of the glass into the bottom. This must be the sand clock, he thought.

'Pedro,' said Rodrigo. 'Captain wants you to show this stowaway how to keep the time.'

Pedro glared down at Tomas. He had a pale face, crooked teeth and tiny eyes. 'A stowaway!' he exclaimed. 'The captain wants me to teach a stowaway the principle of the sand clock. Why?'

'The other clockers are sick,' said Rodrigo. 'This one looks like he'll make a sailor.' He grinned at Pedro. 'He says he stowed away to fight the English.'

Pedro spat. 'A stowaway.'

'I'll leave him with you, then,' said Rodrigo. 'If he gives you any trouble you know where to find me.' Rodrigo held his huge fist up to Tomas's nose. 'You'd better behave yourself, boy, or else.'

When he was gone Tomas studied the sand clock.

'Now listen,' snapped Pedro, grabbing Tomas

by his left ear. 'That is a sand clock. It is the second most important instrument on board ship. It is so important there are three more aboard and spares. I have had two years of experience in servicing and keeping the sand clock so you will obey me.'

'Ohhh,' cried Tomas, as Pedro squeezed his ear tighter.

'You will obey me, isn't that right, boy!' Pedro shouted.

'Ye ... yes,' cried Tomas.

'I will not have you or anyone interfere with keeping the correct time. Do you understand? Do you?'

'Ohh ... yes ... yes ... I understand,' cried Tomas.

Pedro let go. 'Good,' he said as Tomas rubbed his tender ear. 'Now pay attention. Are you listening?' He glared at Tomas.

'Yes,' said Tomas quickly. 'I'm listening. I'm listening.'

'Good. Now the sand runs from the top glass into the bottom. This takes exactly one half hour. The clock must not be turned until the very last grain of sand falls to the bottom. When it does the clock must be turned instantly, so not a second is lost.' Pedro narrowed his eyes. 'You heard what I sang out at the turn of the clock?'

'Yes,' said Tomas.

'You will learn the words,' said Pedro. He studied Tomas. 'Can you write?'

'No, but I have a good memory,' said Tomas. He began. 'One glass is gone, another's a-filling. More sand shall ... shall?'

'Run,' snapped Pedro.

'Run, if God is willing.' Tomas raised his eyebrows for Pedro to help him.

Pedro sighed. 'To my God let us pray.'

'To make safe our way,' said Tomas quickly. He frowned as he tried to remember what came next. 'And his ...?'

'Mother, Our Lady, who ...' Pedro nodded for him to continue.

'Prays for us all, to ...to ...?'

'Save us from tempest.'

'And threatening squall,' said Tomas, grinning. Suddenly his stomach gave a loud rumble.

Pedro frowned. 'Are you hungry, boy? Oh, what is your name anyway?'

'Tomas. Yes, I'm starving.'

Pedro looked at the clock. 'When the next half hour is sung I'll go below and get you a biscuit. It will keep the hunger away until the evening meal.'

'Thank you,' said Tomas as his stomach rumbled again.

Pedro's lip curled. 'Don't thank me. I need you. If the other two useless dolts weren't sick I wouldn't even talk to you. One of them is my brother Julio. He begged me to ask the captain for a position as sand clocker. He let me down. Look, it is my duty to keep the correct time. As chief sand clocker, I and I alone am responsible for keeping the clock shift running smoothly. Nothing must interfere with keeping the correct time. I must make sure it is correct all the way to England and, if we return, all the way back.'

Suddenly the ship gave a violent lurch which almost threw Tomas across the deck. Pedro grabbed him and, holding on with his other hand, he pulled Tomas towards the hand rail, around the clock. The ship rolled back and forth. Pedro studied Tomas. 'Do you think you'll survive what the French call the Mal-de-mer?'

'The what?'

'Seasickness. Are you a good sailor?'

'I ... I don't know,' answered Tomas. 'I've never been to sea before. In fact I'd never seen a ship before yesterday.'

'Never seen a ship,' muttered Pedro. He sighed as he turned to the sand clock.

Tomas looked out to sea again. He smiled as he breathed in the clean fresh air. It was lucky for me that the other sand clockers got sick, he thought. Looking up, he saw several sailors clambering along the masts. The ship pitched, groaned and shuddered, threatening to throw them off. Things couldn't have worked out better, he thought. I'm really on my way to England. He wondered how his cousin was faring below.

5

ON HIS OWN

It was over ten days before Tomas saw his cousin again – ten days in which the weather grew worse. By then almost every soldier was seasick. From Pedro, Tomas learned that many of the soldiers were weak and dehydrated from vomiting and diarrhoea. Pedro also told him his brother and the other sand clocker were still very sick; too sick to attend to their duty.

By now the stench of vomit and diarrhoea was everywhere. Occasionally Tomas would see soldiers come from below and empty buckets of it overboard.

In that first week on board ship Tomas made friends with Pedro. At first Tomas was only able to relieve Pedro for a couple of hours at a time, but soon he was taking longer shifts. Pedro, who wasn't as stern as he appeared, was grateful to Tomas for his help. He soon learned to depend on him.

The day Tomas saw Diego was another stormy one. Tomas was on the four-in-the-evening -to-midnight shift, and it was after six when his cousin and another soldier came up on deck to empty the buckets.

Tomas didn't even recognise his cousin until the

34

wind blew Diego's hair back from his face.

'Diego!' Tomas shouted. 'Diego!'

His cousin looked around, but the roar of the sea and the slashing rain drowned the sound of Tomas's shouts. In a moment Tomas was stumbling across the deck and down the steps. Once he was thrown against the rail bordering the steps and almost banged his head, but somehow he made his way to Diego.

Diego couldn't believe his eyes as Tomas rushed to embrace him. When they parted Tomas stared at his cousin. His face was gaunt and almost as white as the flapping sails. His uniform, creased and stained with vomit, hung on him. He looked like a scarecrow.

'Tomas,' gasped Diego. 'How?' He forced a smile. Tomas saw his teeth were yellow. He also saw the lice crawling through his hair.

'I'm a sand clocker!' shouted Tomas, trying to make himself heard above the crashing waves. His face was covered in spray and his hair was soaking. The ship pitched and groaned as Diego shouted, 'I thought the singing sounded familiar.'

'Are you all right?' shouted Tomas.

Diego attempted another smile. 'No one is all right below. All the soldiers are sick. The only water we have to drink is going green. The food is almost gone and most of it is rotten. Not that any of us can keep it down.' Diego licked his cracked lips and scratched at his hair. 'But what about you? You seem all right.'

'I haven't been seasick,' shouted Tomas, holding

tight to a rope as the ship lurched hard again. He quickly shouted the story of how he had managed to get aboard. When he was finished he asked, 'How long do you think it will be before we get to England?'

'According to the sergeant, another two, maybe three, weeks.' Diego looked at the other soldier, who was retching by the edge of the deck. 'Tomas,' he shouted. 'If the soldiers in the other ships are as sick as we are the English will easily defeat us. Some below are nearly dead. There will be many dead if we've much more of this weather to take.'

'Pedro said the weather should change soon,' said Tomas, hoping the news would cheer his cousin. He still couldn't get over the shock of Diego's appearance.

Diego saw that the other soldier was ready to go below. 'I have to go, Tomas, I'll ...'

Suddenly a shout from above drew their attention.

Tomas gasped. 'It's Pedro. Madre-de-Dios,' he exclaimed. 'I'll see you again, Diego.' He stumbled away.

His cousin watched him for a few seconds, then turned to help his companion below.

'You left your post!' screamed Pedro. His face was red with anger. Sweat ran down his brow.

Tomas frowned. He could understand Pedro being angry at him, but something else was bothering him. Pedro should have been resting. What had wakened him?

'I only left it for a minute, Pedro,' he explained.

'My cousin ...'

'You left your post!' shouted Pedro. 'What if you had fallen overboard or been injured and couldn't get back? What then? The clock would not have been turned. Time would have been lost. I'm responsible for the clock ...'

'But Pedro ...'

'There are no excuses!' shouted Pedro. 'You left your post. You ...' Suddenly he groaned and doubled over.

'Pedro! What's wrong?'

'Tomas ... I ...' With a gasp Pedro pitched forward onto his face and slid along the wet deck.

Tomas stared at him. Blood was pouring from a cut on Pedro's cheek. He was unconscious. 'Help!' he cried. 'Somebody help!'

His cries brought Rodrigo and another sailor.

'He ... he just fell over,' said Tomas.

The ship gave another shuddering groan and Pedro's body slid a bit further along the deck.

'Another one!' shouted Rodrigo. 'Grab him quick!' He glared at Tomas. 'Boy, get back to your duty. We'll see to Pedro.'

Tomas watched as the sailors carried Pedro away. Then he remembered the clock. He was just in time. The last grains of sand trickled into the bottom glass. Quickly Tomas turned it and began to sing out. 'One glass is gone, another's a-filling ...' As he sang he wondered what was wrong with Pedro. He realised that if Pedro was unable to attend to the clock it would be up to him.

On the turn of the next half hour Captain De

Salto came over to Tomas.

'Captain,' Tomas greeted him. He liked the captain and was grateful to him. He turned to look at the clock, aware that the captain was watching him. As he turned the clock and sang out he realised the captain was waiting until he finished.

When he was finished the captain said, 'Tomas, you have done very well.'

'Thank you, sir,' said Tomas, beaming. 'I enjoy being a sand clocker. But,' he added, 'it's to fight the English that I stowed away.'

De Salto smiled, but suddenly his face grew serious. He looked at the other ships, which were strung out as far as he could see. He wondered whether they were in the same predicament he was. If so, the soldiers would not be strong enough to fight babies, never mind the English. When the Armada landed in England they would all be slaughtered. Almost a quarter of his crew were sick, most with stomach cramps and diarrhoea. Any food that remained was not fit to eat. Nearly all the good water had been drunk. He dreaded having to tell his crew and those below that it would have to be rationed. He turned to Tomas again. 'Tomas, Pedro is sick. There is no one to relieve you from your duty. I'm afraid you will have to keep the time until he is better. I don't know how long that will be.' He studied Tomas's shocked expression. 'Do you think you can do your duty alone?'

Without hesitating Tomas answered, 'Yes, sir, I can.'

De Salto smiled. 'Good. I'll convey your faithfulness to your duty to the commander. Well, Tomas, I'll leave you to it.'

Tomas watched him stagger over to the wheel to relieve the first mate. Some day, he thought, I'm going to be a captain of a galleon like this. What adventures I'll have. He smiled as he looked at the other ships.

Then the seriousness of his position hit him. He was the only sand clocker now. Captain De Salto, the commander and Pedro were depending on him. He thought about the captain's words. 'Do you think you can do your duty alone?'

At the same time something crawled onto his brow and he brushed it away. Soon he was scratching hard at his head.

As the ship crashed through the waves Tomas wondered how often he would have to turn the clock before they reached England.

6
TURNING BACK

By the end of the fourth day Tomas was exhausted. Once he almost missed the turn. He would have fallen asleep several times if the lice in his hair had not been driving him mad. The captain had given him a fine wooden comb to comb out the irritating insects, but it was a long task before his hair was free of them. Occasionally Tomas would hear a soldier cry out in frustration about the torturing lice which infested the lower decks. Any soldiers who came on deck were constantly tearing at their hair.

Instead of easing, the storms had grown worse, and during those four days Tomas had seen six ships with broken masts and torn sails falling back for repairs. Two ships had also crashed into each other. One was so badly holed that the crew and the soldiers had to be taken on board other ships. Behind Tomas, helping the first mate keep the ship on an even keel, De Salto fretted. He had never known weather like this. If the storms kept up he knew many below would die. Don Alonso, the commander, had remained in his cabin, and De Salto suspected he too was suffering. Shading his eyes, he looked towards the leading galleon, the flagship *San Martin*. Many of its flags were in tatters. De Salto looked around his own vessel. At least his ship was in good condition, apart from one sail which had torn in half. Another had been quickly hoisted into place and the torn one was nearly repaired. He looked at Tomas as he sang out the half hour, and noted that Tomas's voice was weaker. The boy has done well, he thought. He made a mental note to reward Tomas when they reached England; if they ever reached England.

As if reading his thoughts, Juan, the first mate, yelled, 'Sir, how long are we going to continue like this? Look at the *San Martin*, and the *De Quesa*. They're in a mess. We'll be throwing ourselves at the mercy of the English fleet if we meet them in this condition.'

De Salto sighed. He looked skywards. Even if the storms subsided they would not be ready.

By the end of the following week Tomas was near collapse. He had to be constantly wakened by Rodrigo or another sailor well before the sand ran out. When he had sung out the time he immediately fell asleep again.

But by the beginning of the next week Pedro appeared, looking very weak and even thinner. He insisted on relieving Tomas.

'But, Pedro, I can do it,' objected Tomas. 'You're still sick.'

Pedro smiled, looking at the huge black rings which circled Tomas's tired eyes. 'Tomas, you have done more than enough.' His next words shocked Tomas. 'But now that the Armada is turning back I need to attend to my duty.'

Tomas shook his head. 'Turning back?'

Pedro stared at him. 'I thought you knew. We're heading back; to Spain, to Corunna. We should be there by the end of the week.'

'But ... but why?' Tomas was stunned.

'It would have been foolhardy to continue. With almost every soldier in the Armada sick, we would have been slaughtered. We couldn't have continued for long anyway, with the food and drink being bad. If we had landed in England we would have been taken easily. We ...' Suddenly Pedro swayed. He held his hand to his head and sank to lean against the bottom of the rail.

Immediately Tomas's disappointment was forgotten. 'Pedro, you're still not well enough. I'll stay here until you feel better. Go and lie down for a while.'

Pedro smiled weakly. 'Thanks, Tomas, but I'd rather stay here. I'll be all right in a little while.'

Later they discussed the decision to turn back.

'Do you think the Armada will sail again?' asked Tomas. 'I mean, soon.'

'Most definitely,' answered Pedro, easing his back against the rail. 'As soon as we get fresh water and food and the weather improves, the Armada will sail again.' Pedro gritted his teeth. 'This time I'll not get sick. It was the food, not the sea, that made me sick. I'm a good sailor. I've been out to sea in rough weather like this before, though it didn't last as long.'

Tomas glanced at the clock. The sand had almost run through. He got ready to turn it, but with a grunt Pedro pulled himself onto his feet. 'Tomas,' he said, smiling. 'Let me do it.'

Tomas studied Pedro, then stood to one side.

At the turn of the clock Pedro's voice sang out. He faltered near the end, but he managed to finish the chant. With a gasp he sat down again. 'I'm still a bit weak,' he whispered. 'But a few more turns and I'll be fine.' He saw Tomas yawning. 'Look, Tomas, why don't you go and have a sleep. I'll be all right. I'll have Rodrigo wake you if I need you.'

'Are you sure?' yawned Tomas.

Pedro smiled. 'Yes, I'm sure. Go on.'

Tomas rose to his feet. 'Thanks, Pedro.'

'No, Tomas, thank you.'

As Tomas staggered across the deck he looked out at the other ships. The storms had subsided a little. He wondered whether he would have to stow away when the Armada sailed again. He wondered how his cousin was.

7

A PRESENTATION

When the Armada reached Corunna thousands lined the quay to welcome them. Sailors and soldiers poured from the ships that were able to dock. Others rowed ashore from the many ships that had had to moor out in the harbour.

Tomas waited for Diego. As he watched the soldiers coming up from below, Captain De Salto, Don Alonso – resplendent in his blue uniform – the first mate and Pedro came over to him.

'Tomas,' said the captain. 'Let me introduce you to Commander Don Alonso de Luson. Commander, this is Tomas, the boy I told you about who excelled in his temporary duty as sand clocker.'

The nobleman smiled at Tomas, who blushed at the praise. 'Tomas, Captain De Salto has asked me to present you with these boots as a token of his gratitude for all you have done.'

Tomas stared in amazement at the most beautiful pair of leather boots he had ever seen. The leather, with its fine carving and buckles, shone in the bright sun. For a few seconds he was speechless. Then he could only say, 'Oh, but I couldn't ... I don't deserve ...' He looked at Pedro.

The sand clocker smiled and nodded for Tomas

to take the boots.

'Th ... thank you, sir,' choked Tomas.

Don Alonso smiled. His next words almost made Tomas burst into tears. 'When we sail again, Tomas, I'd consider it an honour if you would be one of my sand clockers on board the *Valencera*.' He turned to Pedro. 'With both of you looking after the sand clock I know I'd have the two best sand clockers in the Armada.'

Pedro blushed and his smile grew wider.

'Now I think it's time we all went ashore,' said the nobleman.

'Oh, and Tomas,' said De Salto. 'Call the paymaster; I've told him to pay you your proper rate. Thank you again.'

As the captain, Don Alonso and Juan walked away, Tomas gazed at his boots.

'It will be a while before they fit you,' said Pedro, smiling.

Tomas held them out to him. 'Pedro, these are yours really. I couldn't take them.'

'Oh, don't be silly, Tomas. Without you on board the sand clock would have lost valuable time. I'm indebted to you too. Come on, let's get ashore. I'll treat you to a glass of Corunna's best wine.'

Tomas looked at the soldiers milling around the lifeboats. 'I have to wait for Diego. But if you don't mind we'll both have a drink with you later.'

Pedro slapped him gently on the shoulder. 'I'll see you on the quay then.' With a smile he walked away.

When Tomas saw Diego he was even more

shocked. His cousin looked even thinner than he had before. Most of the soldiers were in a similar state and still scratching. But they were all in good spirits. Tomas listened as their officer addressed them.

'You are all ordered to report to your ship tomorrow. From there we will be helping to set up camp on the outskirts of Corunna. So enjoy yourselves tonight; there will be plenty for you to do from now on.' The officer looked over the men. 'If any of you are thinking of deserting, remember deserters will be executed. That is all.'

As Tomas hurried to join his cousin, he saw Diego staring at the officer with a strange look in his eyes.

Later, they sat together in the middle of the packed lifeboat as it headed for the quay. Diego whispered to Tomas, 'I'm never setting foot on this or any other ship again. I'm going back home. My father will forgive me.' He looked at Tomas. 'And you.'

Tomas frowned. 'But Diego,' he whispered, glancing around quickly to make sure no one was listening to them, 'you heard the officer. If you desert you'll be executed.'

'I don't care,' whispered Diego. 'I'd rather be shot than get on board a ship again. When I reach the land I'll kiss it. Madre-de-Dios, I've never suffered as much in my life. Many a time I wished I was dead. Working on the farm will be heaven compared to being on a ship again.'

Tomas said nothing. If Diego was going home he

knew he'd have to go as well. They had set out on their adventure together. He could understand how his cousin felt. He wondered whether he would have felt the same way if he had been cooped up below decks. He sighed but then thought hopefully, maybe when we've been ashore for a while Diego will change his mind. But he didn't think it was likely.

The sun shone bright on the white walls and vineyards of Corunna. The town itself was thronged with sailors and soldiers and the many who came to welcome them. Celebrations were going on everywhere, though the sailors and soldiers knew they would be sailing again soon.

When Diego and Tomas reached the quay they were met by Pedro and his brother Julio. Julio was as tall as Pedro but even thinner. He had huge bags under his dark eyes. He smiled at Tomas, saying, 'Pedro has told me how well you have done. It appears I owe you a drink or two.'

'There's a tavern I know further off the quay. I've been there before and they serve good wine and food,' said Pedro. 'A good meal, then we can get a warm bath and get rid of these lice.' He scratched his head. As they followed him Diego and Tomas began to scratch too, though the lice didn't seem to be as troublesome now.

The tavern was packed, but Pedro was able to persuade a serving girl to find them a table in the corner. Tomas watched Diego. His appetite was voracious and he gulped down his food and wine as if it was his last meal. As they ate they talked about when they would be sailing again.

'They're already unloading the barrels and rotten food,' said Pedro. 'Some of the ships are in need of repairs. I reckon that if fresh fruit and vegetables and decent water barrels are found we'll be sailing in about a week. Ten days at the most.'

'Not me,' said Diego. He wiped the grease from his lips and burped loudly.

Pedro looked at Tomas, then asked Diego, 'What do you mean?'

'I mean,' said Diego, reaching for another piece of chicken, 'I'm going home. I've had it with ships. There's nothing on earth will make me get on board one again. Tomas and I belong on my father's farm. We'll never leave it again.'

Frowning, Pedro turned to Tomas. 'Is that true, Tomas? You heard what Don Alonso said. You'll be a sand clocker on the *Valencera*. He asked you.'

Tomas looked down at the new boots he was wearing, then looked at Diego. Then he said quietly, 'If Diego is going home I'll have to go too. We promised to stay together.'

Now it was Diego's turn to frown. 'Tomas, don't you want to go home?'

Tomas shrugged his shoulders. 'No,' he said, looking straight into Diego's face. 'No, I don't. I've never been very happy there. But I was happy at sea. I loved being on the *Valencera*.'

'Then ... then you want to go with the Armada when it sails again?' asked Diego.

'Yes ... yes, but if you're not going ... we promised

48

to stay together, remember,' said Tomas.

Diego frowned. 'Tomas, you don't know what it was like below decks.It ... it was ... I can't go back.'

'The journey will not be as rough this time,' said Julio. 'The admiral will wait for better weather.'

'And the food and water will be better,' added Pedro. 'That's why I was sick,' he said to Julio. 'The food and water – ughh.' He scratched his head. 'And the lice. I need a bath. We all need a bath before the lice eat into our skulls.'

Diego squirmed as he watched Tomas and Pedro scratch their heads. Then Julio was at it. Diego burped again. 'Let's have another bottle of wine. Then we'll see about getting a bath.'

Later, outside the bath house, the boys said goodbye. Pedro, who had an aunt living on the edge of town, gave Tomas the directions on how to get there. 'Just in case you change your mind. My aunt will put us up until the Armada sails again.'

'Thanks, Pedro,' said Tomas. 'I'm going home but I'll never forget you – or you, Julio.'

'Diego,' said Pedro. 'Please think again about joining the Armada. We aren't that far from England ... about eight days with a good wind behind us. The voyage will be shorter.'

Tomas turned hopefully to his cousin. But with a curt 'Goodbye', Diego turned and walked away.

Later still they walked along the quay. Already carts were being loaded with the rotten food and broken barrels. Some of them were already moving away. Hundreds of men ran up and down the gangways getting the ships ready.

'Are we heading home tonight?' asked Tomas an hour later. They were sitting on a low wall at the edge of the town, near a small vineyard.

'No, better to make a fresh start in the morning,' said his cousin.

Tomas sighed.

Diego said, 'Tomas, you weren't really happy on that ship, were you?'

Tomas nodded.

'That's probably because you weren't sick. God, I feel sick just thinking about the smell and the rolling, the endless rolling of the cursed ship.'

'You weren't the only one who wasn't used to the sea,' said Tomas. 'All the soldiers felt like you. Maybe ... maybe when the Armada sails again you won't be sick. And you heard Pedro. He says the journey won't be as long.'

'I don't care what Pedro says,' snapped Diego.

'I thought you wanted to fight the English,' cried Tomas. He was growing angry. 'What about, "We'll be rich? We'll be heroes?" Diego, it was all your idea. Don't tell me you don't want to fight the English any more?'

His cousin glared at him. 'Of course I do; but on land, not on the cursed sea.'

'You have to go to sea to get to England,' snapped Tomas.

'Yes, I know,' Diego snapped back. 'That's the problem.'

'So you're just going to give up and go home!' shouted Tomas.

'Give up? I'm not giving up!' shouted Diego. He

glared at Tomas. 'Are you saying I'm a coward?'

Tomas shrugged his shoulders. 'You're going home, aren't you? You're not going to fight the English. You've given up!'

Diego made a lunge for Tomas and grabbed his arm, but Tomas shook him off. He startled both of them. Tomas could never have done that before the voyage had weakened Diego. 'What's wrong with you?' Diego shouted.

'Nothing! Nothing!' shouted Tomas. 'I know I don't want to go back to your father's farm. There's nothing there for me. I want to go to England and fight the English like we planned. I want to be ... to be a sand clocker.' Tomas turned his face away.

After a long time Diego said, 'Tomas, I'm sorry, but – It's just that I couldn't get on a ship again. Don't ask me to ...'

Tomas sighed. 'No,' he said quietly. 'I won't ask you again.' He looked around. It was a warm starry night. 'Where are we going to sleep?'

Diego pulled off his tunic. 'Why not here, behind the wall. It's a warm enough night.'

As they lay looking up at the stars Diego tried to convince Tomas that going back to the farm was a wise decision. 'When we get home I'll teach you how to shoot with my bow. I'll make you one.' He glanced at Tomas. Tomas's face looked pale. 'We'll get used to the farm,' said Diego. 'You'll see.'

'Will we?' said Tomas quietly. 'Will we see the world working on the farm?'

Diego remembered his own words. 'I don't want to live on the farm all my life. I want to see the world, and the best way to do that is to join the Armada.' He turned away his thoughts to the ship, and shuddered as he remembered how desolate he had felt; how once, before he found out Tomas was on board, he had thought of jumping overboard. He fell asleep thinking, Tomas will feel differently in the morning.

Tomas waited another fifteen minutes before he slowly stood up. There was a lump in his throat as he whispered, 'I'm sorry, Diego.' A few minutes later he was heading back into the town to look for Pedro's aunt's house.

8
SAILING AGAIN

Tomas smiled as he, Pedro and Julio waved to the cheering people gathered along the quay. It was the 21st of July 1588, Tomas's birthday. He was back on the *Trinidad Valencera* and it was one of a hundred and thirty ships sailing again to attack England.

Tomas had thought about Diego often over the past nine days. He still felt guilty about leaving him. He wondered whether Diego had reached home yet.

It was an uneventful and pleasant journey, and eight days later, just before four in the afternoon, the Armada reached the Scilly Isles off the coast of England.

Tomas was on duty as the first isle came into view, and his heart beat faster with excitement when the look-out yelled he had sighted England.

Around six o'clock the first mate drew Captain De Salto's attention. He pointed towards the edge of one of the isles.

De Salto trained his telescope in that direction. He could see a tiny ship racing around the isle. 'I see her,' he shouted. 'Get the commander, Juan!'

Seconds later Don Alonso stood with them, watching the fast English patrol ship disappear.

'It will head straight for Plymouth,' said De Salto. 'We'll sight the English fleet soon.' He smiled as he looked at his sails. 'With this wind behind us we'll sight the coast of England tomorrow.'

The following evening the look-out shouted a warning. 'English ships to starboard!'

Tomas, who had been keeping Pedro company, ran with him to the edge of the deck. They were shocked to see at least ninety English ships about a mile behind them.

'They must have sailed all night to get there,' cursed De Salto, handing the wheel to his first mate.

'What do you think the captain will do?' asked Tomas.

'I don't know,' said Pedro, looking behind him. De Salto had his telescope trained on the ships. 'With the English behind us,' said Pedro, 'and with this wind, they have the advantage. We'll be fighting them soon, I'll warrant.' He looked left and right. 'There's still plenty of room for the Armada to manoeuvre and engage the English fleet, but if we're trapped between them and the English coast, I don't know.' He smiled at Tomas's worried expression. 'Don't worry, Captain De Salto isn't that stupid.'

Four hours later they could see the English fleet clearly. At her head was the biggest ship, bedecked with flags.

'That's the Ark Royal,' shouted Pedro. 'The English Admiral Howard will be aboard.' Pedro studied the English ships.

'They're faster than ours,' he muttered. 'Much faster.'

'Look!' shouted Tomas, pointing. 'The *San Martin* is turning. They're signalling from the Duke's galleon.'

'We're all turning, by the looks of it,' said Pedro, listening to the captain shouting orders. They watched as the sailors scurried around the ship.

'Then we're going to fight?' exclaimed Tomas.

'Looks like it,' said Pedro, glancing at the sand clock. A few seconds later he turned it. As his clear voice sang out, Tomas saw the galleons and galleasses sailing to form a wide semi-circle. He could see that the transport ships had dropped back and now fighting ships sailed quickly in front of them.

'What are they doing?' he asked Pedro.

Pedro studied the strange formation. 'Yes, I think ... yes, the famous Spanish Crescent.'

'The what?'

'The Crescent,' explained Pedro. 'The fastest fighting ships have already moved to the front, see. They'll protect the transport ships.' Pedro held his curved hand out to Tomas. 'They're forming a crescent,' he said, indicating the curve. 'If any of the English ships sail into the Crescent they'll easily be swallowed up and destroyed.' Pedro closed his hand to show Tomas. Then, opening it again, he said, 'The English will only dare attack the ships at each end of the Crescent. If they move any closer they will be surrounded.'

The two sand clockers watched as the Crescent

took on its full shape. From end to end it must have spanned at least six miles. The *Valencera* was near the middle, just in front of a transport ship. Now, as the Crescent held its formation, the English ships closed in to harry the ships at each tip. The sound of pounding cannons grew louder and Tomas and Pedro cheered when they saw the top sail of an English ship ripped to threads.

Suddenly: '*The Ark*!' shouted Pedro, pointing.

They watched as the *Ark Royal* led an attack on the left-hand tip of the Crescent.

'Look at the other end!' shouted Pedro.

Tomas saw a group of English ships attacking the right-hand end.

'I wager Drake is leading their attack,' said Pedro. They turned to watch the *Ark Royal* and other ships engage in furious cannonade; but now Spanish galleons sailed to meet them. The thunder of cannon fire was deafening. Pedro and Tomas could see that the English cannons were firing short while the Armada ships were finding their targets. Pedro turned to see how the other tip of the Crescent was faring. Horrified, he nudged Tomas and pointed. A group of fighting ships had come about to meet Drake's attack. As the Crescent sailed on, two of the biggest galleons had been left isolated. A group of English ships moved to attack them.

'It's the *Gran Grifon*!' exclaimed Pedro. 'See her flag. I can't make out the other ship. Look, the English are closing in on them. They'll be captured.'

The English ships closed in to a range of four hundred yards. As Tomas and Pedro were joined by Julio, they saw that the two galleons were being pounded by cannon fire.

The battle went on for two hours, and all that time Pedro kept up a running commentary. His knowledge of each ship was amazing.

The sand clockers saw the *San Martin*, followed by a group of fighting ships, break from the Crescent and race to rescue the two trapped ships. By now the battle area was so packed, it was hard to see the water, and more fighting ships sailed to join the main battle. Pedro was the first to cheer when he saw the *Ark Royal* move away. The Crescent moved quickly into shape again, and the *Gran Grifon* and the other ship were soon safe within it. Soon the Armada was moving up the English Channel.

Tomas and the brothers couldn't contain their excitement. 'We'll be in London soon,' said Pedro, smiling.

'Did you see the English scatter!' exclaimed his brother.

'Their ships looked faster than ours,' said Tomas.

'They were,' said Pedro. 'But our cannons can shoot further than theirs. Speed isn't much good if you can't get close enough to do damage.'

Tomas turned to look at the captain, the first mate and Don Alonso. All three were smiling. Tomas turned to starboard. The English were still on the Armada's heels as it sailed eastwards.

As thick darkness descended Tomas stood alone

at the clock. His thoughts drifted to Diego. He wondered how he was. He wished Diego had been with him to experience the unforgettable battle he had seen.

That night the wind dropped.

Next morning the Armada crawled through the English Channel to Portland Bill.

As the day wore on, Tomas, who was too excited to sleep, joined Pedro.

'There's no wind,' he exclaimed, looking up at the sails.

'No,' said Pedro, looking at the sky. 'And I don't think we'll get any for a while, by the look of that sky.' He turned to Tomas. 'If the wind does pick up, the next battle will be the one which will decide the war.'

All night the sea remained calm. But at five o'clock a breeze began from the north-east. It was then the English fleet attacked again.

9
Going Home

All that day the noise of cannon fire was deafening. None of the sand clockers felt like sleeping; they were far too excited. But their excitement turned to fear when the *Valencera* was hit. A cannon ball ripped two lifeboats to pieces. The wooden shards killed three sailors and injured five more. A smaller ship near them, the *Gerona*, was holed in the bows and over thirty killed.

Tired, but unwilling to miss any of the battle, the sand clockers took turns singing out each half hour.

By Friday the Armada had forced its way up the channel. It was a lovely cloudless day and not a shot had been fired all day. Tomas wondered why. The Armada still sailed at a slow pace.

Saturday came and still no more cannons had been fired. All the while the English coast had been in sight; but soon the sand clockers noticed they were sailing farther from it.

'France is that way,' said Pedro frowning. 'You can hardly see England any more. I wonder why we're heading for France.'

That evening, with the English fleet a mile behind, the Armada anchored off Calais. The English ships dropped anchor half a mile away.

On Sunday morning the sand clockers learned

that the Armada was to sail against England on Monday morning.

That Sunday night Tomas was on duty. It was a stormy night and the wind whipped at his face as he watched the lanterns on the English ships. When Tomas turned the clock and sang out the half hour he could hear some of the sand clockers on the other ships singing too.

At the first turn of the clock after midnight Tomas noticed a ship with a light coming from where the English had anchored. Suddenly he saw flames erupt from the ship and spread quickly through it. Horrified, Tomas saw the ghostly shapes of other smaller ships. They too were on fire, and the wind was carrying them quickly towards the Armada.

'Fire!' he yelled. 'Fire! Fire!'

Immediately everyone was alerted. Stunned, they saw the fire-ships sailing towards them. With their masts and rigging covered in tar, and every cannon on board ready to fire on its own as soon as the flames reached it, the fire-ships were carried into the closely-moored Armada.

The screaming and the confusion sent shivers up and down Tomas's spine. The flames seemed to be everywhere. The smell of burning tar filled his nostrils. Cannons exploding, timbers cracking with the heat, the fire-ships were gusted straight into the middle of the Armada. The patrol boats tried to get a line to one of the fire-ships, but there were eight others to deal with and it was an impossible task in the gusting wind.

Discipline was forgotten. In a panic, several of the captains ordered their anchor ropes cut to get away. Later it was found that the fire-ships had done little damage; but had achieved what the English fleet had failed to do in earlier battles. They had scattered the Armada.

By dawn a hundred and thirty ships were strung out near the Dunkirk sandbanks. That was when the English fleet attacked. It was impossible now for the Spanish to form their invincible Crescent.

The roar of the cannons and the screams of injured men terrified Tomas. He could see Pedro and his brother were frightened too. He wished he had never left his uncle's farm.

Their terror increased as a cannonball shattered another lifeboat. Now only one lifeboat remained on the *Valencera*.

Another cannonball ripped a hole in the deck – just beside Julio, who was standing near the rail. The force of it threw the sand clocker across the deck, and he landed heavily on his back.

'Stay with the clock!' shouted Pedro, running to Julio. 'I'll carry Julio to the lower deck.'

As Pedro straightened, with his brother in his arms, a cannon ball sailed over him, only a few feet above his head. It screamed over the deck and into a supply ship, killing eight men.

As the day wore on Tomas did his duty and kept a close watch on the battle. He could see that the English were winning.

By four o'clock Captain De Salto gave the order to run, following many other ships who had managed to get out to open water.

Galleons and galleasses drifted in groups of two and three. The Armada was truly scattered.

At six o'clock a squall suddenly rose up, accompanied by heavy rain which had Tomas soaked to the skin in seconds. The ferocity of the squall was such that both fleets withdrew from battle and looked to their own sea safety.

Later, when the wind subsided slightly and Pedro came on duty, he told Tomas that Julio had not regained consciousness.

'Tomas,' Pedro whispered, pointing to the English fleet, nearly a mile away, 'there are more of them. We're defeated. The Armada will be destroyed if we stay to fight.' As he spoke the wind grew stronger, then suddenly changed direction from north-west to south-west. Quickly the captain ordered his sails lofted to take advantage of the wind. Soon all the ships in the Armada began to move out into the North Sea to safety.

Four hours later there was no sign of the English.

'They're lowering a lifeboat!' shouted Pedro, trying to make himself heard above the howling wind.

Twenty minutes later they saw Don Alonso and another officer get into the lifeboat.

'Where are they going?' shouted Tomas.

'I believe they'll have a council of war on the *San Martin* to decide if we are to turn back and try again,' said Pedro.

Tomas's eyes widened. 'Do you think they will?'

'I don't know,' said Pedro. 'There will be some

who will risk their lives to try again. There will be others who will say they will try again when the winds are favourable. I don't know,' he repeated.

Three hours later Don Alonso and the officer returned. The sea was so rough that it took them nearly three quarters of an hour to get aboard. The sand clockers watched the grim-faced nobleman climb unsteadily up the steps and cross the rolling deck.

A few seconds later the captain handed the wheel to his first mate and followed Don Alonso inside.

A cry woke Tomas. Rising, he hurried to Pedro.

'What's happening?' he asked, noticing the full sails.

'We're going home,' said Pedro.

Tomas had no need to ask why. With almost every ship damaged, no ammunition, and no friendly port to pull in to, it was a wise decision. The *Valencera* was taking in water. It was going to be a long journey home – if they ever reached home.

The winds grew stronger. As they reached the tip of Ireland and began to go around it, they came on a galleon called the *San Felipe*. It was sinking fast. On board were forty soldiers and eleven sailors, two noblemen, the captain and the first mate.

Tomas watched as the survivors were pulled aboard. It took almost four hours. As the last two soldiers were hauled aboard Tomas thought one of them looked familiar. It was a moment before he could believe his eyes.

'Diego!' he cried. 'Diego! Diego!'

He fell once on his way down to the lower deck.

As they embraced, Tomas gasped, through tears, 'How? I thought ...'

When they parted Diego smiled as he told Tomas what had happened. 'I decided you were right: there was nothing for me back at the farm. Next day I went to the ship with the other soldiers, and we set up camp on the outskirts of Corunna. But my regiment was assigned to the *San Felipe*. It was too late to do anything then.' His face grew grim. 'Well, Tomas, we'll hardly see London now.'

Tomas sniffed. 'It doesn't matter any more, Diego. We're together again. That's what matters now.'

They embraced again. Remembering the clock, Tomas said, 'I'll try to get down to see you later.' He smiled and hurried away.

As he turned the clock and sang out Tomas felt happier. He watched as the soldiers disappeared below. Diego looks fine, he thought.

A few minutes later Pedro came out. As it was several hours before his shift Tomas was surprised to see him. He frowned. Tears were running down Pedro's thin face.

Tomas gulped. 'Julio?'

'He's dead, Tomas,' cried Pedro. 'My little brother Julio is dead.'

Too stunned to cry, Tomas hugged Pedro. As the wind howled around them, the ship slowly rounded the tip of Ireland.

10
IRELAND

Tomas could see land. Through the wind, mist and crashing waves, high cliffs rose up like ghostly spectres. He gripped the smooth rail as he turned to Pedro.

'Ireland!' he shouted.

'Yes,' said Pedro. 'The captain will be looking for a safe anchorage now. If he doesn't find a sheltered bay we'll sink. The hold's full of water.' He turned to Tomas. 'Can you swim?'

Tomas frowned as he looked at the rolling waves. 'Do you think we'll have to?' He could swim, but he knew his cousin couldn't. Tomas had tried to teach him, but Diego had a terrible fear of water.

'I hope not,' said Pedro. 'I can't.'

Tomas stared at the cliffs. There seemed to be no way up them. He looked down at the crowded lower decks. About a hundred and fifty soldiers were gathered on that side. A few were vomiting; some were wounded; many were so weak they could hardly stand; and all were shivering in the cruel Atlantic wind. Tomas looked for Diego, but couldn't see him. He must be on the other side, Tomas thought, or down below with the injured.

It was September 14th 1588, and the galleon *La*

Trinidad Valencera, the fourth largest ship in the Armada, groaned and creaked as it slowly answered to the helm.

A cry drew the sand clocker's attention, and he saw they were sailing towards a wide bay.

'We'll be safe now, Tomas,' said Pedro, smiling. 'We'll soon be ashore.' He looked at the ship's only remaining lifeboat, hanging over the port side of the forecastle. Pedro didn't want to alarm Tomas, but he knew that if the *Valencera* sank quickly not everyone would be saved. He estimated the lifeboat would take only a dozen men safely.

Pedro turned to look at the captain. De Salto and Juan, the first mate, wrestled with the wheel, trying hard to move the *Valencera* into the correct position for steering into the bay. Beside them, his dark eyes watchful and alert, stood Don Alonso.

Just then Juan shouted something and pointed towards the land.

They could see men on the shore, some standing on the curved beach, others plunging out of the thick bushes that grew down the wide glen surrounding the bay.

Don Alonso clenched his hand around the hilt of his rapier. If the Irish clansmen supported the English Queen, then a hostile army would be ranged on the beach within hours. He had around four hundred men on board – many of them injured or too weak to put up much of a fight if it should come to that. Don Alonso did not want to think that after all they had come through, he and his men might die on foreign soil, far from home.

As the galleon eased into the calmer water of the bay the sick soldiers felt their spirits rise. The *Valencera* anchored about two hundred and fifty yards from shore.

'What now?' asked Tomas.

'The commander will want to see if the Irish people are friendly,' said Pedro, pointing. 'But Tomas, look at the colour of their hair. Some of them are so fair, and some have hair the colour of copper. It must be painted.'

Tomas studied the men on the shore. He had never seen a red-haired man before. I hope they are friendly, he thought. The natives looked fierce: they constantly pointed and gestured towards the ship, and one of the biggest of them raised his spear.

Suddenly a bell sounded and everyone turned. Don Alonso was standing on the top forecastle, with Captain De Salto and an officer, who was called Marcos, beside him. He was a handsome man with a slim moustache.

'Men!' shouted Don Alonso, turning to point to the shore. 'That is the Irish coast. We must land there. Captain De Salto has estimated we have around two days before the *Valencera* sinks. As you can see, the beach is crowded with Irish natives. They appear friendly but we cannot be sure. I intend to send a lifeboat ashore with ten of our best swordsmen and officer Marcos who can speak a little of the Irish tongue. We will need help to get everyone ashore safely. I am hoping that the natives will have some type of craft to help us.'

Pedro looked down at the soldiers. 'We'll need help all right,' he whispered.

Suddenly the ship gave a lurch to one side. A soldier who had been hanging over the side was thrown into the water. Before anyone could get a rope to him he disappeared below. Don Alonso was almost thrown out of the forecastle; the captain grabbed his arm just in time.

The ship was listing to one side. The commander glanced at De Salto. They both knew they had less time than they had thought.

Turning to Marcos, Don Alonso said, 'Choose ten of your best men. Get to shore and try to parley with the natives. Try to make them see we can't stay afloat long.'

At once the officer stumbled away.

Pedro and Tomas watched as the lifeboat was lowered into the water. It took the officer and his soldiers ten minutes to get aboard. Two sailors rowed the lifeboat around the ship and towards the shore. As the boat rowed slowly towards the beach, Tomas wished again that he was back at his uncle's farm.

11

A DROWNING

Everyone, except those too injured to come on deck, watched as the lifeboat headed into the narrow channel that led to the beach. The Irish quickly gathered there to meet it. Some of them jumped into the water and helped to pull the lifeboat ashore.

At least they're not attacking, thought Tomas. He turned to Pedro. 'Do you think they'll harm them?'

'I hope not,' replied Pedro. 'If they do then we're finished. The *Valencera* will sink here and we'll go down with it.'

On shore, Marcos and his men jumped from the boat. Keeping close together, the soldiers kept their hands on the hilts of their swords as they were surrounded by the natives.

The men of the *Valencera*, both on shore and on board, watched breathlessly for any sign of animosity from the Irishmen; but none came. An hour later, the officer and another soldier were on their way back to the ship. Clambering aboard, Marcos ignored the many questions that were shouted at him and hurried to report to Don Alonso.

A few minutes later Don Alonso and the captain

stood on the forecastle.

'The natives have agreed to help us, for a price,' shouted Don Alonso, trying to make himself heard above the howling wind. 'They are members of the O'Doherty clan and I believe we can trust them. They are bringing two of their boats to assist us in getting everyone ashore.'

Tomas smiled at Pedro in relief, but the tall sand clocker frowned and looked at the sky. The wind was changing direction.

Don Alonso continued. 'We should have plenty of time if the weather holds. When the boats arrive the sick and injured will be ferried to shore first. All of you, please help to get them above decks.'

Tomas smiled as he spotted Diego, waving to him. His cousin had a wide smile on his face.

But just as Don Alonso finished speaking, De Salto noticed the wind had changed. Later, when the injured were being brought above, he mentioned this to Don Alonso.

The nobleman sighed as he looked towards the shore. He hoped the wind wouldn't get any stronger. He wanted to reach shore with as strong a force as possible. Don Alonso knew the O'Dohertys were by no means unsympathetic to their cause, but he also knew their chief, Sir John O'Doherty, was untrustworthy. Many of those natives hated the English; but they also feared them.

A cry from the lookout alerted him. Two small boats were being rowed out to the ship.

'They'll not be able to take many in those frail

craft,' said Pedro.

But by midnight ninety-three men had been ferried safely ashore.

That night the wind picked up and the sea grew rougher. All next day, as the wind roared and the mountainous waves threatened to dash the *Valencera* to pieces, the lifeboat and curraghs worked hard, and around two hundred men were landed safely. The soldiers stood around several chests and boxes of provisions, protecting them.

Tomas was glad to see that Diego was safely ashore. He could see that the main body of soldiers were more than enough to defy the Irish, if they should attack.

Next day the storm grew worse. At eight o'clock in the morning the lifeboat sank and nine men were drowned. Now only the curraghs were left. Tomas and Pedro, along with Don Alonso, Captain De Salto and the others, crowded to the side of the ship, anxious to get ashore. When one of the curraghs returned, Don Alonso, Captain De Salto and Juan decided they would be next to get aboard. By now the *Valencera* was being pounded by the biggest waves De Salto had ever seen. Because of this, it took them almost half an hour to get on board.

Almost as soon as the curragh was clear of the ship, a massive wave hit the *Valencera*. Wood splintered, canvas ripped, and with a loud crack the huge ship turned over. Tomas and Pedro and some of the others were thrown into the water; but as the ship sank it carried over twenty men to the bottom with it.

Don Alonso, seeing the ship sinking, ordered the curragh to return to pick up any survivors.

In the cold water Tomas struggled to stay afloat. His boots had filled with water. One came off and sank to the bottom. The other was pulling Tomas under. With his bare foot he tore at it. His frantic kicking pulled off the oversized boot. Choking as he swallowed mouthfuls of water, Tomas tried to see around him. He was aware of others struggling for life. Then the curragh came closer and hands grabbed him and hauled him aboard.

It was then Tomas remembered Pedro.

'Pedro!' He stared around him. There was no sign of Pedro. There was no sign of anyone in the water. 'Pedro.'

Someone whispered, 'He's gone, Tomas.'

Tomas turned. 'Gone?'

It was Captain De Salto. His face was grim as he stared at the disintegrating ship. 'Aye, and over forty good men as well.'

'Forty ...' gasped Tomas, shivering. Pulling off his coat, De Salto placed it over Tomas's shoulders. Still shivering, the shocked boy began to cry.

When they reached the shore the natives gathered around Don Alonso. They seemed to be fascinated by the nobleman's garments. Some of them tried to touch him, but soldiers rushed forward and forced them back.

'Bring the chest,' Don Alonso said to one of the crewmen.

Four men who appeared to be the Irish leaders

pushed their way through the crowd to stand in front of Don Alonso. Marcos who had bargained with the tribesmen indicated that these were the men who would receive the gold. Soon a bag of gold coins and a bright cloak of the finest Spanish cloth exchanged hands. The natives seemed satisfied.

Don Alonso studied the area. They were at the bottom of a wide glen with a narrow path winding up it. The nobleman knew that if they stayed where they were they could easily be trapped. He knew they would find help somewhere in the north of Ireland: clans there were sympathetic to the Spanish cause. He wondered whether there were English forces in the area. He had no doubt that if there were, word would be on its way to them. He toyed with the idea of quickly marching inland until they could find a castle; but he knew there would be no comfortable quarters for his men there, and security would be short-lived if there were English forces in the area. The only help was to the north. He decided to march northwards and hope they did not encounter any large resistance.

Soon they were marching out of the glen and through the rough countryside.

Tomas, with Captain De Salto's coat still wrapped around him, marched beside Diego. Diego did not try to talk to his cousin; he knew Tomas had been deeply shocked by Pedro's death. Although Diego, too, had been shocked and frightened by their adventures, he felt much happier now that they were on dry land.

Two hours later Diego saw Tomas falter. One of his feet was bleeding.

'Tomas, are you all right?' he asked.

'What?' said Tomas stupidly.

'Your foot – it's bleeding,' said Diego.

'Bleeding?' Tomas stared at his foot. Blood was oozing from a cut under his big toe.

Diego looked ahead. 'I think we'll be stopping soon. I'll bandage it for you when we stop.'

An hour later they came out of a valley into a flat, boggy area. As they did the whinny of horses drew their attention. A company of English cavalry faced them, already spread out in battle formation.

12

BETRAYAL

At Don Alonso's command, the soldiers drew their swords and quickly spread out. His officers, priming their guns, moved to stand just behind him.

The English cavalry, a hundred and fifty men strong was led by Richard and Henry Hovenden, followers of Hugh O'Neill, Earl of Tyrone. They were an impressive force. Pulling on the reins and kneeing his white horse in the side, a pale, bearded man forced it forward a few steps. The horse whinnied its annoyance and stamped its feet. Its dark eyes glared at the survivors.

'Lay down your weapons!' the bearded man shouted in Spanish.

Don Alonso narrowed his eyes as he studied the cavalry. The nobleman stood with his legs apart, his rapier held to one side. At first he had been ready to fight, but he quickly realised that his march to the north would be impossible if they were continually harassed by the horsemen. He knew his soldiers could hold off the cavalry but not defeat them. He feared the arrival of a larger English force.

'We will never surrender!' he shouted.

Tomas glanced at Diego. His cousin was paler

than usual.

The white horse neighed loudly as the leader of the cavalry shouted, 'Lay down your weapons and you will not be harmed.'

'No!' shouted Don Alonso, taking a step forward. 'We will never surrender,' he repeated.

Both men glared at each other; then suddenly the horseman roughly pulled his horse's head around and trotted back to his men.

Everyone watched him dismount. Several other horsemen dismounted and gathered around him.

'I think we're going to fight,' whispered Diego.

Tomas gulped. He had no weapon and his foot was throbbing painfully.

An hour passed and nothing happened. During that time Don Alonso had time to reflect on his position. He was not insensible to peaceful overtures, but he was not prepared to surrender without ensuring that his men would be safe.

He knew by now reinforcements would have been sent for, but he doubted that there were any nearby; if there had been, they would already have arrived. He looked around. What a desolate place this Ireland is, he thought. He longed for the warmth of Spain. Making up his mind, he turned to his officers. 'It doesn't look like we're going to fight yet. Make provisions ready for half the men. The other half are to stay alert.'

Suddenly a group of five horsemen rode up. Don Alonso and the survivors watched as they quickly dismounted and conversed with the other dismounted horsemen.

Occasionally these five strangers – who were not cavalry men – took long looks at the Armada survivors.

'What are they up to, Commander?' whispered Marcos. 'Why don't they attack?'

Don Alonso turned. 'Do you think they would be wise to?'

The officer thought quickly. 'No, we would defeat them.'

'Yes, but at what cost?' said Don Alonso, turning. He saw a tall, heavy man with a black beard mount his horse and ride towards them.

Behind him the nobleman felt his soldiers tense.

The horseman stopped about twenty-five yards from Don Alonso. He had grey-flecked hair and wore a tunic made of animal hair.

'Hear me,' he began, in broken Spanish. 'I am Hugh O'Donnell of the O'Donnell clan. I have been asked to arrange a meeting between your leader and Major Kelly, who is the officer in charge of the cavalry.'

Don Alonso frowned. He knew the O'Donnell clan were opponents of English rule. If this man was truly an O'Donnell he could be trusted.

'Come closer!' he shouted.

Tomas, Diego and the others saw the man slowly walk his horse forward and stop about ten yards from Don Alonso.

'Are you truly an O'Donnell?' he asked.

'Sir,' replied O'Donnell, 'you have my word I am. I fear for your safety. That is why I have come to set up this meeting. If you cannot come to some arrangement with the Major you will be cut down. There are upwards of a thousand troops on their way here.'

'A thousand ...'

Don Alonso heard the dismay behind him. Quickly he made up his mind. 'Very well, I will parley with this Major Kelly.' He looked around. Thick bushes grew at the edge of a nearby bog. Pointing, he said, 'We will meet at yonder bushes. His cavalry are to move back, as will my soldiers. I want you and the Major and no one else, to meet me and one officer.'

'And the time?' asked O'Donnell, looking steadily at the nobleman.

'At first light,' replied Don Alonso, thinking, it will give my men time to rest. 'Now ask the Major to withdraw his men.'

O'Donnell smiled. He glanced again at the soldiers, then spun his horse about and rode back to the cavalry.

Don Alonso waited until he saw the cavalry move back about a hundred yards. Then he turned to address his men. 'You all heard. I am to parley with this Major Kelly at first light. I do not trust him; but the O'Donnell clan are sympathetic to our cause and I believe I can trust this Hugh O'Donnell. Now let us set up camp.'

Later, as Diego bathed Tomas's foot, Tomas said, 'I wish we had stayed on the farm after all.'

Diego sighed. 'I wish I had gone home when I had the chance.' Suddenly he smiled. 'Ah, Tomas, we're together. That's what matters. We'll survive.

If we survived the storms at sea we'll survive anything.' He smiled again when Tomas suddenly yawned. 'You're tired.'

'Yes.'

'Why don't you get some sleep? Lie down. I'll cover you with the captain's coat. It will keep you warm.'

Tomas yawned again. 'Diego,' he whispered, 'I'm sorry I convinced you to go back to the army.'

'Oh, Tomas, I wanted to but I didn't know it then. I suppose if I had to do it again I would.' He smiled. 'You worry too much. Now get some sleep.'

Tomas tried to smile, but as he lay back his thoughts drifted to Pedro and Julio. Pedro had told him how he dreaded having to tell his parents Julio was dead. Who would tell them now? Who would tell Diego's parents if they were killed?

Later Diego shivered as he looked at Tomas. His cousin was fast asleep. They had come a long way. His mind drifted to his parents and his sisters. He missed them. He felt a tear run down his face as he thought, I'll never see them again.

The shouting woke Tomas. It had rained in the night, and with no shelter to protect them, everyone had been soaked to the skin. Tomas shivered. His feet were freezing.

Now he saw what had woken him. Don Alonso and another officer were walking towards the bushes. Hugh O'Donnell and Major Kelly, who was a small man with a clean-shaven face, were waiting for them.

Cavalry and soldiers watched as the four stood, hands on the hilts of their weapons, and conversed.

Major Kelly spoke through O'Donnell, brusquely demanding that Don Alonso and his soldiers give up their weapons and surrender. The Major promised them safe conduct to Dublin.

Don Alonso refused and turned away; it was a bluff, but O'Donnell stopped him with the words, 'What are your terms for surrender?'

Don Alonso had his answer ready. 'I will surrender if you give me your word as an O'Donnell that we will have safe conduct to Dublin. In addition, each private soldier and crewman must be allowed to keep one suit of apparel, and each officer two suits. Then we will lay down our weapons.' He held O'Donnell's gaze. 'Do I have your word?'

O'Donnell smiled. 'You have my word.' He turned to Kelly. 'And the Major's.'

So it was decided.

At midday, in a wide field beside a bog-land, Don Alonso surrendered his arms. Swords, small firearms, and pikes were handed over. When this was done the horsemen dismounted and moved among the Spanish, separating the officers from the ordinary soldiers.

'Tomas, I don't like this,' whispered Diego. 'Look, they're leading Don Alonso and the officers away.'

Tomas frowned. 'Perhaps they're going to parley again.'

Diego shook his head. 'The time for parleying is

over. The English have the advantage now.' He looked around. 'We're helpless,' he whispered. 'Helpless.' Suddenly he grew afraid. 'Tomas, move into the middle of the soldiers.'

Tomas stared at him. 'Why?'

'Do it,' snapped Diego, staring at the cavalry men, who were mounting their horses. 'Follow me.'

They were no sooner within the group of soldiers than one of them shouted, 'Look, the English are drawing their swords!'

'They're going to fire!' screamed another.

A volley of musketry rang out. Only a few feet from Tomas, two soldiers cried out and collapsed; one turned as he fell, and Tomas saw the gaping hole in his chest.

'Run!' screamed Diego. 'Tomas, run for your life! They're charging!'

Tomas froze, unable to take in what was happening. As another soldier fell, mortally wounded, Diego pulled at him. 'Run, Tomas!' he screamed. 'We've been betrayed! Run!' A horseman ploughed through the soldiers, swinging his sword wildly; Tomas ducked and the sword which would have decapitated him scythed into another soldier's neck. Shuddering, the soldier fell to the ground. Another horseman raced at Tomas, but with a curse Diego leapt at him and pulled him from his horse. He smashed his fist into the horseman's face. He shouted to Tomas, 'Run! Get away from here! Run!'

In a moment Tomas had turned and was running

across the field, towards the bushes which bordered the bog-land. Behind him he could hear musket shots and screaming and shouting, and the terror of what was happening drove him on. Crashing through the bushes, he was sure he heard a horseman behind him. Seconds later he was in the bog. Behind him he heard Diego cry out, 'Tomas!' He ran faster into the soggy ground. Not daring to look back, Tomas choked and cried out as he stumbled and fell on his face. In an instant he was on his feet again and heading deeper and deeper into the bog.

13
A Village

Tomas didn't know how far he had run. Both his feet were bleeding and he was cold and soaked through with rain. He had not looked back once.

Two hours later he collapsed near some fuchsia bushes. He lay there shivering, his teeth chattering loudly. He tried to think about what had happened. The English had opened fire and cut down the helpless survivors. 'Diego,' he choked. Diego was dead, just like Pedro and Julio. 'As long as we're together we'll be all right.' 'We were together!' screamed Tomas. 'We were ...' He began to cry. 'Oh Diego ... Diego ...'

An hour later he slowly stood up. He realised the English would be looking for him and any others who had escaped. The ground Tomas had run through had been soggy and once he had sunk up to his thighs in the brown earth. He realised that the bog had saved him. The horsemen couldn't drive their horses into it without risking injury to their mounts. Tomas wondered again how many of the others had got away.

He stared ahead. In the misty distance he could see a valley between two mountains. He decided to make for it. I might find some shelter there, he thought, and maybe some food. Shivering, he began to trudge towards it.

When he was about half a mile from the valley he spotted two men coming along another narrow path to his left.

Tomas dropped to the ground but it was too late: the men had seen him. The smallest of them shouted and they began to run towards him. Jumping to his feet, Tomas began to run back the way he had come. His heart was pounding with fear as he tried to outrun the men. By their attire he knew they were Irish – each wore a sort of blanket garment. Glancing back, Tomas saw they were catching up. The tallest of them had long black hair which flapped around his face giving him a wild look.

If he hadn't been so weakened by shock and cold, Tomas might have had a chance of outrunning the men, but suddenly he stepped into a deep hole. His momentum carried him forward and he hit his face on the ground. Stunned, he tired to scramble to his feet, but by then the men were running up to him.

One of the men said something in a strange language – the only word Tomas recognised was 'Spain' – and reached out to touch Tomas's coat. The other man struck his hand away, and the two began to argue.

Tomas couldn't understand what they were arguing about, but he decided to make a break for it. In an instant he was on his feet and running.

It was a futile effort. The fleet-footed men quickly caught him. This time the taller man reached for the captain's coat. Tomas struggled but the big man pulled it off him and flung him to the ground. Now wearing only a light tunic and shirt, Tomas stared at the men as they began to argue again. Both men had their hands on the coat and were tugging at it. Tomas rose to get away again, but the bigger man punched him on the side of the head. With a low groan he lost consciousness.

When he woke it was dark. His head throbbed and his feet were numb with cold as he struggled to stand up. The wind whipped his wet hair back from his face as he squinted in the darkness. A little way ahead he saw the glow of a fire. Tomas knew that if he stayed where he was he would die of exposure. He stumbled towards the fire.

It took him all of twenty minutes. On the way he stumbled into a shallow pool of water, and the coldness made him cry out with pain and frustrated anger. Now he lingered, shivering, on the edge of a small village. He could see the silhouettes of several round dwellings. He could smell cooking, and the thought of something to eat made his mouth water. In the glow of the fire he could see dark figures moving about.

He moved closer. As he did a dog barked. Trembling with both fear and cold, Tomas crouched down and moved closer, his eyes fixed on the fire. He could almost feel its heat. As he drew closer he saw a young girl lift a pot off the fire and carry it into the nearest dwelling.

All of a sudden Tomas's head spun and he almost fell. He was shivering so violently he hoped the villagers couldn't hear his chattering teeth.

He was about to creep closer when the dog barked again. Tomas heard voices and saw figures emerging from the dwellings. He almost turned back, but he knew that if he ran back into the bog he would die. Better to take the chance, he thought, and stumbled into the light of the fire. All of a sudden he felt faint. 'Help me,' he croaked. 'Help...' As he fell he lost consciousness.

When he woke he was lying on a bed of rushes. He looked around the straw hut he was lying in. Hearing a noise, he turned. A young girl wearing a blanket-type garment stared at him. She had shoulder-length brown hair and piercing blue eyes, and her face was dotted with freckles. Tomas had never seen anyone like her before. Feeling the stiffness in his body, he sat up. He stared at the girl as she handed him a bowl with some milk in it. Without thanking her, Tomas began to drink it. When he looked up he saw the girl was smiling.

She said something in her strange language.

Tomas frowned.

'I ... I don't understand you.'

The girl tapped her chest. 'Maeve.'

Now Tomas understood. He smiled. 'Tomas,' he said, tapping his chest. 'Tomas.'

'Tomass,' said the girl, smiling again. She pointed at him. 'Tomass.' She tapped her chest again. 'Maeve.' She handed Tomas a piece of oaten bread. 'Ith, Tomass.'

Smiling, Tomas took the bread from her. He wolfed it down and drank another bowl of milk. When he looked up the girl was gone.

He looked around the hut. The floor was strewn with rushes and a blanket covered the narrow door. Feeling much better, though his feet still throbbed, Tomas slowly rose to his feet. It was only then he noticed they had been bathed. When he reached to pull the blanket back from the door, a little blood oozed from his toe as he put his weight on it.

As Tomas stepped outside, the biggest dog he had ever seen leapt at him. Both Tomas and the dog landed inside the hut. The dog's teeth glistened as it stood over him, growling.

14
RODRIGO

A red-haired man with a bushy beard shouted at the wolfhound and grabbed it by the back of its neck. In one easy movement he flung the yelping animal outside.

Tomas stared up at him as the man said, 'Spáinn?'

Gulping, Tomas nodded. He knew that if the man decided to kill him he wouldn't have a chance. The man had muscled arms and bare feet; like every Irishman Tomas had encountered, he wore an animal-hair coat and hose-type trousers.

Tomas heaved a sigh as he saw Maeve peek from behind the man. She was smiling. Tomas guessed by the likeness that the man was Maeve's father. Grinning, the man reached a hand down to Tomas. The grip was firm as the man hauled Tomas to his feet. It was only then Tomas realised how tall the man was.

Other men and women and some children gathered around him as he came outside. Tomas could see he was in a village of about a dozen straw huts, spread over an area of about half an acre. The women wore smocks and blankets. Some of the older women wore handkerchiefs folded tightly over their heads and fastened in front. Some of the natives had red hair; others had black or brown hair. Among them Tomas recognised the two men who had attacked him. One of them was wearing the captain's coat. Without thinking, Tomas pointed at him and shouted, 'That's my coat!'

Maeve's father stared at Tomas. 'Cad é?' He stared at the man Tomas had pointed to.

'That's my coat!' shouted Tomas, pulling at his thin shirt sleeve.

Maeve's father, who Tomas guessed was the leader, glared at the black-haired man. 'An leis an buachaill an cóta?'

The man scowled and pulled the coat tight around him.

Tomas could see the men were arguing about the coat. Maeve's father strode towards them.

'Tabhair dom é,' he snapped. He straightened to tower over the small dark man, who looked at his companion, but seeing he was on his own glared at Tomas.

'Tabhair dom é!' shouted the leader.

The smaller man, his upper lip curling with anger, pulled the coat off and threw it at the leader's feet.

Tomas looked at Maeve. She smiled at him.

Maeve's father, with his eyes still on the dark man, picked up the coat and walked back to Tomas. He handed it to him.

'Thank you,' said Tomas, and pulled it on.

Maeve's father studied him for several seconds.

'Tomass,' said Maeve, pointing to Tomas.

'Tomass,' said her father, smiling. He tapped his

chest. 'Owen.' Then he turned to a red-haired woman near him and gave her some order.

The woman hurried to the nearest hut. Tomas gasped when he saw the man the woman led outside. His gold earrings glistened in the sun.

'Rodrigo!' shouted Tomas, running towards him. It was only when he felt the sudden pain in his feet that he almost fell. He limped towards the sailor.

Rodrigo stared at him. His left arm hung limply by his side. Tomas could see the deep lacerations on his forearm.

The natives watched as Tomas hugged the big sailor gently. Rodrigo quickly explained how he had escaped. He had taken a different route from Tomas. He had killed a horseman who had pursued him and had been wounded during the fight. 'Well, stowaway, we've landed ourselves in a fine fettle.'

'Did ... did you see Diego?' asked Tomas. He was almost afraid to ask.

'Diego?' asked Rodrigo.

'My cousin,' said Tomas. 'He's a soldier.'

Rodrigo sighed. 'Nearly all the soldiers were slaughtered. If your cousin was a soldier I doubt if he survived.' He spat and cursed. 'The cowardly English.'

'What are we going to do now?' whispered Tomas.

Rodrigo stared at him. 'Avoid getting caught by the English,' he said. 'And find some way to get back to Spain.'

'Spain? But how?'

'Boy, if I knew that I'd do it. But I'll tell you, I'd rather die trying to get back home than live in this accursed land.' He spat again, then suddenly grimaced as he felt his arm. 'We were lucky, boy. Extremely lucky. These natives could have been loyal to the English and handed us over.' He looked over at Maeve's father, who was arguing with the two bearded men. 'We'll have to somehow convince them to help us get home.' He stared between the mountains. 'We're near the sea. If we can get to the coast we'll have a better chance of finding a seaworthy craft to get home one.' He studied Tomas. 'I noticed you limping. If we head for the coast I don't want you holding me back.'

'I'll be all right,' said Tomas. His feet were stinging, but he said nothing.

Owen came over to them. He pointed between the mountains, saying something in his own language.

'No use trying to understand their accursed language, boy. It's a waste of time. We'll have to hope we come on one of these natives who can speak our tongue.' Rodrigo nodded at Maeve's father and said, smiling, 'He looks like a great bear, doesn't he?'

Tomas sighed. He looked at Maeve, who smiled at him, then turned bashfully away. How long are we going to have to stay here? he thought.

15
THE STRANGERS

For the next five days Maeve looked after Tomas and Rodrigo. Every day she bathed Tomas's feet, and every evening she brought them food – Tomas and Rodrigo soon realised that the Irish only ate one meal a day. Tomas grew to like the girl; he wished he could understand her language.

Rodrigo grew more restless. He grumbled all the time. One afternoon he told Tomas he was heading for the coast early the next morning. Tomas knew his feet were much better. He told Rodrigo he would go with him.

That night Tomas was awakened by Maeve. She held one hand over his mouth; with her other hand she signalled to him to be quiet. Tomas could hear shouting outside. When he heard the neighing of a horse he almost cried out with fear.

'Ná Sasanaigh,' whispered Maeve.

Tomas shook Rodrigo awake. 'Rodrigo,' he whispered. 'The cavalry are here.'

Rodrigo scrambled to his feet. In a moment they were all peering out of the door. By the light of the dying fire they could see the silhouettes of men and horses.

Maeve tugged on Tomas's sleeve and beckoned them to follow her.

Slipping behind huts, they followed the girl away from the village. Maeve led them quickly along a path to the foot of one of the mountains. Beckoning them to follow her, she led them up a winding shingle path. As they climbed, Tomas and Rodrigo took occasional looks back at the village. In the fire's glow they could still see the dark shapes and hear English voices shouting.

Twenty minutes later Maeve brought them to a place overhung with thick bushes. Before pulling back the bushes she looked back to make sure they had not been followed. Hidden within the bushes Tomas and the sailor could see a damp cave. Maeve nodded for them to go inside.

When their eyes grew accustomed to the darkness they saw some rushes heaped on one side of the floor. Maeve spread them out and they sat down. When she saw they were settled, Maeve signed to them that she was going away and that she would be back later. Then she disappeared into the darkness outside. Tomas shivered as she pushed the bushes back into place.

Later, as they lay trying to get to sleep, Tomas noticed that Rodrigo was very quiet. He realised the sailor had been frightened. They had nearly been caught. Tomas knew if the English had caught them they would have been killed at once. He thought about Diego. Maybe Diego had been lucky.

An hour later he was fast asleep. In the middle of the night he woke Rodrigo by screaming Diego's name. It was near dawn before he got back to sleep.

In the morning Maeve returned. 'Tar,' she said, smiling at Tomas. She beckoned them to follow her.

They had only been back at the village an hour when they heard the sound of galloping horses. They ran to the door, but they could see no sign of the horsemen.

A few minutes later Maeve and her father came for them. Owen beckoned them to follow him. Tomas looked at Maeve. She smiled and he knew it was all right.

They followed Maeve and her father to the biggest hut in the village. As the approached they saw two horses eating grass outside the hut.

Rodrigo studied them. 'Boy,' he whispered, 'can you ride?'

Tomas realised what Rodrigo meant. 'No,' he whispered, his heart pounding at the thought. 'But I could learn.'

Rodrigo nodded and put his forefinger to his lips, telling Tomas to be quiet. They followed Owen and Maeve inside.

The two strangers in the hut were obviously related; brothers, Tomas thought. One was almost bald; the other, younger, man was going bald. Both the men had bushy beards and dark eyes. They were similarly dressed in hose, rough boots and animal-hair tunics. Their wet over-garments were hanging near the fire. Tomas later found out the bald one was called Patrick and the younger man, Neil. Both Rodrigo and Tomas saw that Neil had a pistol stuck in his belt.

Patrick stood up. He reached to shake Tomas's and Rodrigo's hands. Neil sat studying them.

'You will be found if you stay here,' said Patrick in broken Spanish. 'The English are everywhere. You must get to Doire. You will get help there.'

'Doire?' said Rodrigo. 'Where's that?'

The man frowned. His eyes widened as Rodrigo repeated his question. He held up his hands, indicating on his fingers the number of miles.

'Bishop O'Gallagher help ... Spanish get ... home,' said Patrick.

Smiling, Rodrigo turned to Tomas. 'Did you hear that?' he exclaimed. Turning back to Patrick, he asked, 'Where is this Bishop?'

'Doire,' answered the bald man, looking at Tomas.

'But where is Doire?' asked Rodrigo, thinking, This native is stupid.

Patrick frowned again, then held up his ten fingers. 'Doire must be ten miles away,' said Rodrigo, turning to Tomas. He turned back to the man. 'You will take us to the Bishop?'

Patrick smiled. He glanced back at his brother, who smiled too. The bald man's next words made Rodrigo and Tomas frown.

'Gold,' he said, holding out his hand.

'Gold!' exclaimed Rodrigo. 'But I have none.' He turned to Tomas. 'Have you any gold?'

'No ... I ...'

Rodrigo swung back to Patrick. He held his hands face up. 'No gold. No gold.'

Patrick smiled. 'Gold,' he said, pointing at

Rodrigo's ears.

The big sailor's eyes widened. 'My earrings no!'

The bald man's smile disappeared. 'No gold ... no Bishop ...no help.'

Rodrigo scowled. He knew he would have to part with his earrings. Reaching up, he pulled one open, then slipped it through the lobe of his right ear. He handed it to Patrick, who then indicated the other earring.

'You'll get it when we get to Doire and see the Bishop,' said Rodrigo.

Patrick's eyes narrowed. He turned to his brother, then back to Rodrigo. 'Gold!' he shouted.

Rodrigo feared that if he gave the man his last earring they would have no bargaining power. 'When we get to the Bishop you'll get it,' he snapped. Rodrigo knew if the man insisted he would have to give it to him.

Patrick glared at him. He rose to his feet, saying, 'We ...go ... now.'

Rodrigo and Tomas couldn't contain their excitement at the thought that they were going to be taken to the Bishop of Doire, and he would help them get home.

He said something and Tomas turned to Patrick, 'What did he say?'

Patrick shrugged, 'He said you will always be safe in his village if you cannot return to your homeland.'

Tomas smiled at Owen, 'Thank you,' he said.

The villagers gathered around them. Tomas saw Maeve standing on the edge of the crowd. Tears brimmed in her eyes. Tomas smiled at her and mouthed the words 'Thank you'. Owen shook their hands.

'We'd ... better go now,' said Patrick. He looked beyond the village. 'Horsemen will not ... be ... far ... away.'

A few minutes later, with Tomas sitting behind Patrick and Rodrigo sitting behind Neil, they rode out of the village. As they passed a rocky path between some bushes Tomas saw Maeve again. He waved. 'Goodbye, Maeve!' he shouted.

'Slán agat, Tomass!' she called.

Maeve stood amongst the bushes until they were out of sight. Then, with a sigh, she headed back into the village.

Soon they were approaching Doire. After riding for miles along flat, muddy lanes, they began to climb a steep hill. Once the horse Rodrigo was sitting on stumbled, and the sailor fell off and slid a couple of yards down the hill. Cursing with pain, he scrambled to his feet, slipped and fell again, then managed to grab hold of the horse's tail with his good hand. In this way, they made their way on up. Near the top, Rodrigo, with Neil's help, managed to pull himself onto the horse again.

As they crested the hill the sun broke through the white clouds and they saw Doire. The whole valley stretched away below them. The river encompassed Doire on all sides and a bog divided it from the mainland. They could see a windmill to their right; higher up there was a rough rectangular clay and stone fort, with a tiny church near the middle of it. Away to their left they could see another church. The city was surrounded by oak trees; a few houses and cottages and many straw huts could be seen among the trees.

Pointing, Patrick said, 'Bishop Réamann O'Gallagher lives ... there.' Tomas and Rodrigo saw a tiny house not far from the church.

'Gold,' said Patrick, reaching out his hand to Rodrigo.

Rodrigo scowled. 'Take us to the Bishop first.'

Suddenly Neil gave Rodrigo a shove; the sailor slid off the horse and landed with a heavy thud on the ground.

Neil drew his pistol. At the same time Patrick pushed Tomas and he was thrown to the ground as well.

'Gold!' screamed Neil, pointing the pistol at Rodrigo, who still lay on the ground.

Though he was angry, Rodrigo wasn't stupid enough to argue with a man who was pointing a pistol at him. Cursing under his breath, he pulled the earring off and threw it at Neil. As quick as lightning, Neil caught it. He studied it, then bit it. He seemed satisfied. With a shout of triumph, he kneed his horse into a gallop.

Rodrigo scrambled to his feet and he and Tomas watched as the men rode back down the hill. When they were out of sight, Tomas and Rodrigo turned to look at the Bishop's house.

'I hope he'll help us,' said Tomas as they began walking down into Doire. He hoped the two men hadn't been lying about the Bishop.

16
THE BISHOP

It took Tomas and Rodrigo nearly fifteen minutes to reach the house. It was not as grand as they had thought it would be; it was not much bigger than the big hut in the village where they had met Patrick and Neil.

The hollow sound of Rodrigo's knock on the oak door echoed inside. The door opened a few seconds later to reveal an old woman. Her hair was almost white and she wore a black shawl.

'Bishop's house?' said Rodrigo.

The woman looked him up and down.

'Bishop's house?' repeated Rodrigo.

She shook her head.

Rodrigo looked at Tomas. It was obvious the woman couldn't understand them.

'Bishop's house,' said Rodrigo again.

It was then the old woman realised. 'Is as an Spáinn iad,' she exclaimed. She looked past them, then beckoned them inside.

The cold paved floor made Tomas's feet ache as the woman indicated they were to wait by the low fire. She hurried into another room. When she returned she brought with her a stern-faced man whose hair was whiter than hers. The Bishop was a tall man with piercing dark eyes and pale skin;

he was dressed in the same simple attire as the villagers.

'How did you get here?' he asked in perfect Spanish, and his smile changed his appearance.

Rodrigo and Tomas relaxed, glad they could be understood. 'Two men, Patrick and Neil, brought us on their horses,' said Rodrigo.

'The O'Hegarty brothers,' said the Bishop. 'You're lucky you reached my house. Those two scoundrels have robbed more of your countrymen than I can count, though they've never harmed them.' The Bishop studied Tomas, who was shivering. 'Here, move closer to the fire. You both must be hungry. I'll have Missus Muldoon get you something to eat; then I'll take you to the others.'

'Others?' said Tomas.

'Yes. About twelve of your countrymen from the *Valencera* reached Doire safely. They had terrible tales to tell of being attacked by English troops.'

Tomas and Rodrigo nodded.

'Look,' said the Bishop, 'I have to go over to St. Augustine's to supervise the building of the altar. I'll be back in an hour. Then I'll take you to the others. And have no fear – you'll be quite safe here.'

When he had gone Tomas thought about the others. Might Diego be one of them?

When the Bishop returned he brought two blankets with him. He handed them to Tomas and Rodrigo, saying, 'Wear these. We are going out and I don't want too many people to see you. There are some in Doire who would betray you.'

The Bishop took them along the river bank until

they came to a dense wood of tall oaks. He led them quickly through the trees; on the far edge of the wood they came to a small cottage.

As they approached it, four soldiers standing outside gave a start, but when they saw the Bishop they relaxed and called to the others in the cottage.

Tomas's heart beat faster as all the soldiers and sailors came outside. There were eleven soldiers and three sailors, but Tomas could hardly hide his disappointment: Diego wasn't one of them.

Tomas began to question them about his cousin. One of the soldiers said, 'We were much too terrified to pay heed to anyone else. We were all lucky to escape alive. And if His Excellency has news of our passage home we'll be luckier still.'

'I have,' said the bishop. 'I wanted to wait until you were all together.'

As the men gathered around him, he said, 'I have arranged for a small craft to take you to Killybegs, a fishing village in Donegal. There is a galleon being repaired there ...'

'This galleon,' interrupted Rodrigo. 'Do you know what it is called?'

'I think it is called the *Girona*,' replied the Bishop.

'The *Girona*,' said Rodrigo, smiling. 'I sailed on her once. She is one of the biggest ships in the Armada.' He frowned. 'Is the fishing village far from here?'

'Towards the west of Donegal,' said the Bishop. 'You will all sail down the River Foyle, the river that runs through Doire, then out and around the headland to Donegal Bay. The captain of the vessel has been instructed to take you into Killybegs harbour in O'Donnell country. You'll be safe there.'

'O'Donnell country,' exclaimed Tomas. 'But it was an O'Donnell who betrayed us.'

'Aye, Hugh O'Donnell,' said Rodrigo. He spat. 'Our commander said the O'Donnell clan could be trusted, but he betrayed us.'

'I see,' said the Bishop. 'Then your commander couldn't have known the O'Donnell clan are split. Some of them would support the English.'

'And these O'Donnells in Killybegs?' said a soldier.

'You'll be safe there,' said the Bishop. 'You have my word on that.' He smiled. 'Now I would suggest you get some sleep. You'll be sailing tonight after dark.' He turned to Rodrigo and Tomas. 'You two were lucky you arrived when you did.'

Yes, thought Tomas. But what about Diego? If I do get back to Lisbon, how can I tell my uncle his son is dead? He felt a lump in his throat as he thought again about Diego's words: 'As long as we're together we'll be all right.'

Near dark the Bishop and a priest came for them. In the cold darkness the clergymen led the survivors back along the river. Tomas was surprised to see how fast the river was.

Two small sailing ships were tied to the wooden quay. As they hurried up the gangway of the first ship, Tomas looked back. He could see a few lights from the fires of the few houses which lay along the steep banks of the river. He looked down at the water; it looked cold and unwelcoming. It was beginning to rain again. At home Tomas had loved it when the rains came. Here it seemed to do nothing but rain.

In the deck of the boat the Bishop said a prayer to Our Lady for a safe journey. As he prayed, the rain grew heavier and a loud crack of thunder shook the boat. The flash of lightning lit up the river and the Bishop's pale face. Tomas studied the Bishop. He was risking his life by helping them. If the English found out, the Bishop would surely be executed.

They all lined the deck and waved to the clergymen. 'God bless you!' shouted the Bishop. His shout was followed by the captain's: 'Cast off!'

Soon they were sailing down the Foyle. Half an hour later they were into Lough Foyle and sailing quickly on.

They huddled together, too excited to sleep. Tomas listened to a soldier called Gomez talking about the Bishop.

'I saw him once in Barcelona a few years back. He was with a group of priests. They had just been to see King Philip. Even then Bishop O'Gallagher was known to everyone. I heard the English have tried to trap him more than once, but he has always managed to thwart them. We were lucky the *Valencera* sank near Doire.'

Not so lucky, thought Tomas, thinking again about his cousin.

17
KILLYBEGS

By morning they were sailing out around the headland and moving quickly towards Donegal Bay.

It was a bright gusty day and they made good progress. Earlier they had had a good breakfast of fresh fish, oaten bread and milk, and everyone was in good spirits.

It was around six o'clock in the afternoon when they rounded the headland and sailed into Killybegs harbour. Almost at once they saw the *Girona* moored in the middle of the harbour. The sixteen survivors cheered as they drew near her. When they were alongside, an officer on board shouted, 'Take your boat to the quay. There's no room on board yet; not until the repairs are finished.'

As the boat sailed towards the quay, Tomas could see it was packed with hundreds of soldiers and sailors. Most were standing near the edge of the quay; others were lounging against some wooden buildings nearby.

A short time later Tomas and the others were helped onto the quay. As Rodrigo looked around, he whispered to Gomez, loud enough for Tomas to hear, 'There are too many.'

'What do you mean?' asked Gomez, looking around.

'I mean the *Girona* won't be able to carry everyone,' answered Rodrigo.

'Where did they all come from?' asked Tomas as they pushed through the crowd.

'From other wrecked ships, of course,' said Rodrigo. He began to speak to two sailors, who told him the galleon they had been on had sunk and all but eleven men had been drowned.

'When do you think the *Girona* will be ready to sail?' asked Gomez.

'Not for at least two weeks,' said Rodrigo. 'Did you see the mast? It's cracked all the way down. Aye, two weeks or longer if they have to replace the mast. I'll bet the steering is damaged too. No, not for at least two weeks.'

As Tomas followed Rodrigo and Gomez he looked around. Many of the soldiers were injured. Some of them just stood staring, in a trance. One young sailor screamed and began to convulse. Several soldiers held onto him until he calmed down.

Near the wide lane down to the quay, a group of officers were arguing with several Irish people, who were standing by two carts filled with fresh vegetables and loaves of bread. Tomas and the two sailors watched as the officer in charge bargained with the villagers. A small bag of gold coins changed hands and the other officers shouted to some soldiers nearby to distribute the food. As the soldiers hurried to do as they were ordered,

Rodrigo asked one of the officers, 'How long do you think it will be before the *Girona* sails?'

The officer looked at Rodrigo with distaste. 'Long enough to make all of us poor, with the prices these Irish charge for food,' he snapped. He studied Rodrigo. 'What galleon did you sail on?'

'The *Trinidad Valencera*,' answered Rodrigo.

'How many survived?' asked another officer.

'Sixteen.'

'Sixteen more,' said the officer. 'That makes over eleven hundred.' He narrowed his eyes as he said to Rodrigo, 'Do you think the *Girona* can sail with eleven hundred men aboard?'

The big sailor turned to look at the galleon bobbing up and down in the harbour. 'Maybe,' he said quietly. 'It will be a tight squeeze, but yes, she could take eleven hundred men, maybe even another fifty.'

Tomas thought the ship looked tiny. He was not sure whether Rodrigo was right. He listened as the sailor asked, 'Where can we bed down for the night?'

The officer stared at him. The other officer laughed. 'Bed down? You can bed down where you are. There's nowhere else.'

Just then a group of around eighty soldiers and sailors came pushing down the lane past them. The officer sighed. 'More to feed.' He stopped one of the men. 'How many of you are there?'

Later, as Tomas, Rodrigo and Gomez lay on the hard ground beyond the quay, Tomas thought again about all he had gone through. He wondered whether Don Alonso and Captain De Salto were still alive. He wondered how many ships had been wrecked.

It was a warm night. Somewhere on the quay, a sailor began to sing. His soft voice sang of a lost love, and many sailors and soldiers had tears in their eyes when he finished.

Late in the night Tomas had a dream. He was on the *Girona* and it was sailing into a giant black rock. All around him, sailors and soldiers were screaming in terror as the waves crashed into the galleon, pushing her towards the rock.

But it was the figure standing on the rock, beckoning the galleon towards it, who frightened Tomas. It was Diego. His ghostly face was smiling. The screams grew louder and Tomas awoke, trembling. He lay awake the rest of the night.

18
ABOARD AGAIN

Over the next three weeks the weather improved. Work on the mast was completed, but the more difficult work on the keel and the steering was causing problems. And all the while more survivors were arriving. Now there were over fifteen hundred men gathered near the quay. Tomas worried if he would be one of the fortunate ones allowed on board. He worried also about going home without his cousin. Diego is dead, he thought and a coldness crept over him.

The following week, word spread quickly that the *Girona* was sailing. Everyone crowded the quay. It had long been obvious to all that some would have to be left behind. Still more survivors were arriving. There were now almost sixteen hundred.

On the 15th October the *Girona* was towed to the quay. Everyone moved closer to the galleon. Tomas stood beside the other three surviving sand clockers hoping he would be one of the lucky ones. He was surprised to see two of them appeared ill. The thinnest of the two and the oldest was constantly vomiting. The other boy was mumbling to himself and staring vacantly down at the ground.

Early that evening the noblemen were allowed on board. Now the officers had the unenviable task of choosing who would sail. One of the officers, a young man with high cheek bones and a small scar over his right eye, studied the sand clockers when the four of them were called forward. He stared for a few seconds at the boy who was mumbling to himself then moved to Tomas. He hardly looked at Tomas before moving to study the other two boys. Quickly he made up his mind.

'You,' he said pointing to the boy standing beside the ill sand clocker. 'And you,' he said pointing to Tomas.

Tomas heaved a sigh of relief. He didn't have time to say anything to the two unlucky sand clockers before the officer told them to get aboard and see to the sand clock.

By mid-morning on the 16th of October 1588, there were thirteen hundred men packed aboard the *Girona*. The others lined the quay to see them off.

Tomas, standing on deck beside the sand clock with another sand clocker, could clearly see the quay and the lane leading down to it. Many of the men, both on shore and on board, had tears in their eyes.

Rodrigo, Gomez and four other sailors gripped on thick ropes getting ready for the command to hoist the sails.

'Hoist the sails!' shouted the captain.

As the sails were quickly pulled into place and ropes secured, Tomas, who was still looking towards the quay, saw two soldiers walking down the lane. He frowned as he studied the men. One of them, the smaller, looked familiar, though he had a bandage around his head, covering one eye. Tomas's heart began to pound. Then, as the wind filled the sails, he shouted. 'Diego! Diego!'

The soldier stopped. 'Tomas!' Diego tried to shout again but his throat was too dry.

'Diego, are you all right?' shouted Tomas.

Diego choked out, 'Goodbye ...' Then, clearing his throat, he shouted, 'Goodbye, Tomas!'

The *Girona* was moving away from the quay.

'Diego!' cried Tomas. He looked down at the water. No, he thought. 'No! I can't go. I can't go without him ...'

'Boy!' shouted the captain, seeing Tomas climb over the deck rail.

By now the ship was sailing out into the harbour. Everyone ashore saw Tomas get ready to leap into the water.

'Tomas, no!' shouted Diego. 'No!'

But Tomas leapt from the galleon. As the chilling water closed around him he half-regretted his decision. Spluttering, he surfaced and began to swim towards the quay. Someone threw down a rope and he grabbed it. Seconds later he was climbing the steps. Diego was waiting for him at the top. Watched by some of the curious soldiers, Tomas and Diego hugged each other. Tears ran down their faces.

'Are ... are you all right, Diego?' asked Tomas when they parted.

'I'll not be as handsome as I was,' said Diego, smiling. 'But yes, I'm all right. And you?'

Smiling back, Tomas nodded.

They turned to watch the *Girona* move out into the open sea.

'Tomas, you're a fool,' said Diego. 'You know that, don't you?'

Tomas sniffed. 'All I know is I couldn't go back without you, Diego.'

They hugged again. As they turned to watch the *Girona* sail out of sight, Tomas said, 'As long as we're together, Diego. We'll be all right.'

His cousin smiled. 'Yes,' he said quietly. 'Together.'

The clouds moved in quickly and a wind began to gust. 'They'll be in Spain soon,' said a sailor near them. 'Aye, and they'll send a galleon back for us,' said another sailor.

It began to rain heavily as the cousins walked up the lane away from the quay towards the higher ground. As they walked onto the grass at the top of the lane to make their way across a field, Tomas thought about all they had come through: stowingaway on the *Valencera*, the battle in the English channel, the fire-ships, Julio and Pedro's deaths and all that had happened in Ireland. He sighed as he turned to his cousin.

'Diego do you think we'll ever see home again?'

Diego shook his head. 'I don't know, Tomas. If the *Girona* reaches Spain they'll send a Galleon for us. When that will be, God knows. The English will soon find out the rest of us are here. They'll come.

We'll never be safe. Not here, anyway.'

As they came to the edge of the field, Tomas smiled. He was thinking they would be safe at Maeve's village. There would be other villages.

From the edge of the field above the rocks they had a good view of the bay. Far out they could just see the *Girona* struggling against the wind.

'This Ireland is a strange country,' said Diego when the *Girona* was out of sight and they turned to go back down. 'It was a long hard journey to get here, wasn't it.'

'Yes,' said Tomas thinking again about Pedro and his brother and the others who hadn't made it. 'A long journey.'

Three days later the galleon *Girona* sank off Dunluce Castle near the Giant's Causeway. All but a few were drowned.